PENGUIN BOOKS

BROADWAY STORIES

Damon Runyon was born in Kansas in 1884 and grew up in Pueblo, Colorado. As a teenager he wrote articles for the local newspapers and in 1898, at the age of fourteen, enlisted in the Spanish–American War. He returned to work on various newspapers and became a sportswriter for the New York *American* in 1911. During the First World War he was a war correspondent for the Hearst newspapers and after the war continued to work as a Hearst columnist. He died in 1946.

Runyon's stories are famous for their individual style and grew out of his knowledge of the amiable low-life of Broadway and the New York sporting scene. They were published over a number of years and first collected in *Guys and Dolls* (1932). His other collections of stories include *Blue Plate Special* (1934) and *Take It Easy* (1938). Together with Howard Lindsay he wrote a play, *A Slight Case of Murder* (1935). Many of his stories were made into successful film and stage productions, including the hit musical, *Guys and Dolls*.

DAMON RUNYON

Broadway Stories

PENGUIN BOOKS

PENGUIN BOOKS

Published by the Penguin Group
Penguin Books Ltd, 27 Wrights Lane, London W8 5TZ, England
Penguin Books USA Inc., 375 Hudson Street, New York, New York 10014, USA
Penguin Books Australia Ltd, Ringwood, Victoria, Australia
Penguin Books Canada Ltd, 10 Alcorn Avenue, Toronto, Ontario, Canada M4V 3B2
Penguin Books (NZ) Ltd, 182–190 Wairau Road, Auckland 10, New Zealand

Penguin Books Ltd, Registered Offices: Harmondsworth, Middlesex, England

This collection first published in Penguin Books 1993
10 9 8 7 6 5 4 3 2 1

Penguin Film and TV tie-in edition

Typeset by Datix International Limited, Bungay, Suffolk
Set in $9\frac{1}{2}/12$ pt Monophoto Plantin
Printed in England by Clays Ltd, St Ives plc

Contents

Sense of Humour

One night I am standing in front of Mindy's restaurant on Broadway, thinking of practically nothing whatever, when all of a sudden I feel a very terrible pain in my left foot.

In fact, this pain is so very terrible that it causes me to leap up and down like a bullfrog, and to let out loud cries of agony, and to speak some very profane language, which is by no means my custom, although of course I recognize the pain as coming from a hot foot, because I often experience this pain before.

Furthermore, I know Joe the Joker must be in the neighbourhood, as Joe the Joker has the most wonderful sense of humour of anybody in this town, and is always around giving people the hot foot, and gives it to me more times than I can remember. In fact, I hear Joe the Joker invents the hot foot, and it finally becomes a very popular idea all over the country.

The way you give a hot foot is to sneak up behind some guy who is standing around thinking of not much, and stick a paper match in his shoe between the sole and the upper along about where his little toe ought to be, and then light the match. By and by the guy will feel a terrible pain in his foot, and will start stamping around, and hollering, and carrying on generally, and it is always a most comical sight and a wonderful laugh to one and all to see him suffer.

No one in the world can give a hot foot as good as Joe the Joker, because it takes a guy who can sneak up very quiet on the guy who is to get the hot foot, and Joe can sneak up so quiet many guys on Broadway are willing to lay you odds that he can give a mouse a hot foot if you can find a mouse that wears shoes. Furthermore, Joe the Joker can take plenty of care of himself in case the guy who gets the hot foot feels like taking the matter up, which sometimes happens, especially with guys who get their shoes made to order at forty bobs per copy and do not care to have holes burned in these shoes.

But Joe does not care what kind of shoes the guys are wearing when he feels like giving out hot foots, and furthermore, he does not care who the guys are, although many citizens think he makes a mistake the time he gives a hot foot to Frankie Ferocious. In fact, many citizens are greatly horrified by this action, and go around saying no good will come of it.

This Frankie Ferocious comes from over in Brooklyn, where he is considered a rising citizen in many respects, and by no means a guy to give hot foots to, especially as Frankie Ferocious has no sense of humour whatever. In fact, he is always very solemn, and nobody ever sees him laugh, and he certainly does not laugh when Joe the Joker gives him a hot foot one day on Broadway when Frankie Ferocious is standing talking over a business matter with some guys from the Bronx.

He only scowls at Joe, and says something in Italian, and while I do not understand Italian, it sounds so unpleasant that I guarantee I will leave town inside of the next two hours if he says it to me.

Of course Frankie Ferocious's name is not really Ferocious, but something in Italian like Feroccio, and I hear he originally comes from Sicily, although he lives in Brooklyn for quite some years, and from a modest beginning he builds himself up until he is a very large operator in merchandise of one kind and another, especially alcohol. He is a big guy of maybe thirty-odd, and he has hair blacker than a yard up a chimney, and black eyes, and black eyebrows, and a slow way of looking at people.

Nobody knows a whole lot about Frankie Ferocious, because he never has much to say, and he takes his time saying it, but everybody gives him plenty of room when he comes around, as there are rumours that Frankie never likes to be crowded. As far as I am concerned, I do not care for any part of Frankie Ferocious, because his slow way of looking at people always makes me nervous, and I am always sorry Joe the Joker gives him a hot foot, because I figure Frankie Ferocious is bound to consider it a most disrespectful action, and hold it against everybody that lives on the Island of Manhattan.

But Joe the Joker only laughs when anybody tells him he is out of line in giving Frankie the hot foot, and says it is not his fault if Frankie has no sense of humour. Furthermore, Joe says he will not only give Frankie another hot foot if he gets a chance, but that he will give hot foots to the Prince of Wales or Mussolini, if he catches them in the right spot, although Regret, the horse player, states that Joe can have twenty to one any time that he will not give Mussolini any hot foots and get away with it.

Anyway, just as I suspect, there is Joe the Joker watching me when I feel the hot foot, and he is laughing very heartily, and furthermore, a large number of other citizens are also laughing heartily, because Joe the Joker never sees any fun in giving people the hot foot unless others are present to enjoy the joke.

Well, naturally when I see who it is gives me the hot foot I join in the laughter, and go over and shake hands with Joe, and when I shake hands with him there is more laughter, because it seems Joe has a hunk of Limburger cheese in his duke, and what I shake hands with is this Limburger. Furthermore, it is some of Mindy's Limburger cheese, and everybody knows Mindy's Limburger is very squashy, and also very loud.

Of course I laugh at this, too, although to tell the truth I will laugh much more heartily if Joe the Joker drops dead in front of me, because I do not like to be made the subject of laughter on Broadway. But my laugh is really quite hearty when Joe takes the rest of the cheese that is not on my fingers and smears it on the steering-wheels of some automobiles parked in front of Mindy's, because I get to thinking of what the drivers will say when they start steering their cars.

Then I get talking to Joe the Joker, and I ask him how things are up in Harlem, where Joe and his younger brother, Freddy, and several other guys have a small organization operating in beer, and Joe says things are as good as can be expected considering business conditions. Then I ask him how Rosa is getting along, this Rosa being Joe the Joker's ever-loving wife, and a personal friend of mine, as I know her when she is Rosa Midnight and is singing in the old Hot Box before Joe hauls off and marries her.

Well, at this question Joe the Joker starts laughing, and I can see that something appeals to his sense of humour, and finally he speaks as follows:

'Why,' he says, 'do you not hear the news about Rosa? She takes the wind on me a couple of months ago for my friend Frankie Ferocious, and is living in an apartment over in Brooklyn, right near his house, although,' Joe says, 'of course you understand I am telling you this only to answer your question, and not to holler copper on Rosa.'

Then he lets out another large ha-ha, and in fact Joe the Joker keeps laughing until I am afraid he will injure himself internally. Personally, I do not see anything comical in a guy's ever-loving wife taking the wind on him for a guy like Frankie Ferocious, so when Joe the Joker quiets down a bit I ask him what is funny about the proposition.

'Why,' Joe says, 'I have to laugh every time I think of how the big greaseball is going to feel when he finds out how expensive Rosa is. I do not know how many things Frankie Ferocious has running for him in Brooklyn,' Joe says, 'but he better try to move himself in on the mint if he wishes to keep Rosa going.'

Then he laughs again, and I consider it wonderful the way Joe is able to keep his sense of humour even in such a situation as this, although up to this time I always think Joe is very daffy indeed about Rosa, who is a little doll, weighing maybe ninety pounds with her hat on and quite cute.

Now I judge from what Joe the Joker tells me that Frankie Ferocious knows Rosa before Joe marries her and is always pitching to her when she is singing in the Hot Box, and even after she is Joe's ever-loving wife, Frankie occasionally calls her up, especially when he commences to be a rising citizen of Brooklyn, although of course Joe does not learn about these calls until later. And about the time Frankie Ferocious commences to be a rising citizen of Brooklyn, things begin breaking a little tough for Joe the Joker, what with the depression and all, and he has to economize on Rosa in spots, and if there is one thing Rosa cannot stand it is being economized on.

Along about now, Joe the Joker gives Frankie Ferocious the hot foot, and just as many citizens state at the time, it is a mistake, for Frankie starts calling Rosa up more than somewhat, and speaking of what a nice place Brooklyn is to live in – which it is, at that – and between these boosts for Brooklyn and Joe the Joker's economy, Rosa hauls off and takes a subway to Borough Hall, leaving Joe a note telling him that if he does not like it he knows what he can do.

'Well, Joe,' I say, after listening to his story, 'I always hate to hear of these little domestic difficulties among my friends, but maybe this is all for the best. Still, I feel sorry for you, if it will do you any good,' I say.

'Do not feel sorry for me,' Joe says. 'If you wish to feel sorry for anybody, feel sorry for Frankie Ferocious, and,' he says, 'if you can spare a little more sorrow, give it to Rosa.'

And Joe the Joker laughs very hearty again and starts telling me about a little scatter that he has up in Harlem where he keeps a chair fixed up with electric wires so he can give anybody that sits down in it a nice jolt, which sounds very humorous to me, at that, especially when Joe tells me how they turn on too much juice one night and almost kill Commodore Jake.

Finally Joe says he has to get back to Harlem, but first he goes to the telephone in the corner cigar store and calls up Mindy's and imitates a doll's voice, and tells Mindy he is Peggy Joyce, or somebody, and orders fifty dozen sandwiches sent up at once to an apartment in West Seventy-second Street for a birthday party, although of course there is no such number as he gives, and nobody there will wish fifty dozen sandwiches if there is such a number.

Then Joe gets in his car and starts off, and while he is waiting for the traffic lights at Fiftieth Street, I see citizens on the sidewalks making sudden leaps, and looking around very fierce, and I know Joe the Joker is plugging them with pellets made out of tin foil, which he fires from a rubber band hooked between his thumb and forefinger.

Joe the Joker is very expert with this proposition, and it is very funny to see the citizens jump, although once or twice in his life Joe makes a miscue and knocks out somebody's eye. But it is all in fun, and shows you what a wonderful sense of humour Joe has.

Well, a few days later I see by the papers where a couple of Harlem guys Joe the Joker is mobbed up with are found done up in sacks over in Brooklyn, very dead indeed, and the coppers say it is because they are trying to move in on certain business enterprises that belong to nobody but Frankie Ferocious. But of course the coppers do not say Frankie Ferocious puts these guys in the sacks, because in the first place Frankie will report them to Headquarters if the coppers say such a thing about him, and in the second place putting guys in sacks is strictly a St Louis idea and to have a guy put in a sack properly you have to send to St Louis for experts in this matter.

Now, putting a guy in a sack is not as easy as it sounds, and in fact it takes quite a lot of practice and experience. To put a guy in a sack properly, you first have to put him to sleep, because naturally no guy is going to walk into a sack wide awake unless he is a plumb sucker. Some people claim the best way to put a guy to sleep is to give him a sleeping powder of some kind in a drink, but the real experts just tap the guy on the noggin with a blackjack, which saves the expense of buying the drink.

Anyway, after the guy is asleep, you double him up like a pocketknife, and tie a cord or a wire around his neck and under his knees. Then you put him in a gunny sack, and leave him some place, and by and by when the guy wakes up and finds himself in the sack, naturally he wants to get out and the first thing he does is to try to straighten out his knees. This pulls the cord around his neck up so tight that after a while the guy is all out of breath.

So then when somebody comes along and opens the sack they find the guy dead, and nobody is responsible for this unfortunate situation, because after all the guy really commits suicide, because if he does not try to straighten out his knees he may live to a ripe old age, if he recovers from the tap on the noggin.

Well, a couple of days later I see by the papers where three Brooklyn citizens are scragged as they are walking peaceably along Clinton Street, the scragging being done by some parties in an automobile who seem to have a machine gun, and the papers state that the citizens are friends of Frankie Ferocious, and that it is rumoured the parties with the machine gun are from Harlem.

I judge by this that there is some trouble in Brooklyn, especially as about a week after the citizens are scragged in Clinton Street, another Harlem guy is found done up in a sack like a Virginia ham near Prospect Park, and now who is it but Joe the Joker's brother, Freddy, and I know Joe is going to be greatly displeased by this.

By and by it gets so nobody in Brooklyn will open as much as a sack of potatoes without first calling in the gendarmes, for fear a pair of No. 8 shoes will jump out at them.

Now one night I see Joe the Joker, and this time he is all alone, and I wish to say I am willing to leave him all alone, because something tells me he is hotter than a stove. But he grabs me as I am going past, so naturally I stop to talk to him, and the first thing I say is how sorry I am about his brother.

'Well,' Joe the Joker says, 'Freddy is always a kind of a sap. Rosa calls him up and asks him to come over to Brooklyn to see her. She wishes to talk to Freddy about getting me to give her a divorce,' Joe says, 'so she can marry Frankie Ferocious, I suppose. Anyway,' he says, 'Freddy tells Commodore Jake why he is going to see her. Freddy always likes Rosa, and thinks maybe he can patch it up between us. So,' Joe says, 'he winds up in a sack. They get him after he leaves her apartment. I do not claim Rosa will ask him to come over if she has any idea he will be sacked,' Joe says, 'but,' he says, 'she is responsible. She is a bad-luck doll.'

Then he starts to laugh, and at first I am greatly horrified, thinking it is because something about Freddy being sacked strikes his sense of humour, when he says to me, like this:

'Say,' he says, 'I am going to play a wonderful joke on Frankie Ferocious.'

'Well, Joe,' I say, 'you are not asking for advice, but I am going to give you some free, gratis, and for nothing. Do not play any jokes on Frankie Ferocious, as I hear he has no more sense of humour than a nanny goat. I hear Frankie Ferocious will not laugh if you have Al Jolson, Eddie Cantor, Ed Wynn and Joe Cook telling him jokes all at once. In fact,' I say, 'I hear he is a tough audience.'

'Oh,' Joe the Joker says, 'he must have some sense of humour somewhere to stand for Rosa. I hear he is daffy about her. In fact, I understand she is the only person in the world he really likes, and trusts. But I must play a joke on him. I am going to have myself delivered to Frankie Ferocious in a sack.'

Well, of course I have to laugh at this myself, and Joe the Joker laughs with me. Personally, I am laughing just at the idea of anybody having themselves delivered to Frankie Ferocious in a sack, and especially Joe the Joker, but of course I have no idea Joe really means what he says.

'Listen,' Joe says, finally. 'A guy from St Louis who is a friend of mine is doing most of the sacking for Frankie Ferocious. His name is Ropes McGonnigle. In fact,' Joe says, 'he is a very dear old pal of mine, and he has a wonderful sense of humour like me. Ropes McGonnigle has nothing whatever to do with sacking Freddy,' Joe says, 'and he is very indignant about it since he finds out Freddy is my brother, so he is anxious to help me play a joke on Frankie.

'Only last night,' Joe says, 'Frankie Ferocious sends for

Ropes and tells him he will appreciate it as a special favour if Ropes will bring me to him in a sack. I suppose,' Joe says, 'that Frankie Ferocious hears from Rosa what Freddy is bound to tell her about my ideas on divorce. I have very strict ideas on divorce,' Joe says, 'especially where Rosa is concerned. I will see her in what's-this before I ever do her and Frankie Ferocious such a favour as giving her a divorce.

'Anyway,' Joe the Joker says, 'Ropes tells me about Frankie Ferocious propositioning him, so I send Ropes back to Frankie Ferocious to tell him he knows I am to be in Brooklyn to-morrow night, and furthermore, Ropes tells Frankie that he will have me in a sack in no time. And so he will,' Joe says.

'Well,' I say, 'personally, I see no percentage in being delivered to Frankie Ferocious in a sack, because as near as I can make out from what I read in the papers, there is no future for a guy in a sack that goes to Frankie Ferocious. What I cannot figure out,' I say, 'is where the joke on Frankie comes in.'

'Why,' Joe the Joker says, 'the joke is, I will not be asleep in the sack, and my hands will not be tied, and in each of my hands I will have a John Roscoe, so when the sack is delivered to Frankie Ferocious and I pop out blasting away, can you not imagine his astonishment?'

Well, I can imagine this, all right. In fact when I get to thinking of the look of surprise that is bound to come to Frankie Ferocious's face when Joe the Joker comes out of the sack I have to laugh, and Joe the Joker laughs right along with me.

'Of course,' Joe says, 'Ropes McGonnigle will be there to start blasting with me, in case Frankie Ferocious happens to have any company.'

Then Joe the Joker goes on up the street, leaving me still laughing, from thinking of how amazed Frankie Ferocious will be when Joe bounces out of the sack and starts throwing slugs around and about. I do not hear of Joe from that time to this, but I hear the rest of the story from very reliable parties.

It seems that Ropes McGonnigle does not deliver the sack

himself, after all, but sends it by an expressman to Frankie Ferocious's home. Frankie Ferocious receives many sacks such as this in his time, because it seems that it is a sort of passion with him to personally view the contents of the sacks and check up on them before they are distributed about the city, and of course Ropes McGonnigle knows about this passion from doing so much sacking for Frankie.

When the expressman takes the sack into Frankie's house Frankie personally lugs it down into his basement, and there he outs with a big John Roscoe and fires six shots into the sack because it seems Ropes McGonnigle tips him off to Joe the Joker's plan to pop out of the sack and start blasting.

I hear Frankie Ferocious has a very strange expression on his pan and is laughing the only laugh anybody ever hears from him when the gendarmes break in and put the arm on him for murder because it seems that when Ropes McGonnigle tells Frankie of Joe the Joker's plan, Frankie tells Ropes what he is going to do with his own hands before opening the sack. Naturally, Ropes speaks to Joe the Joker of Frankie's idea about filling the sack full of slugs and Joe's sense of humour comes right out again.

So, bound and gagged, but otherwise as right as rain in the sack that is delivered to Frankie Ferocious, is by no means Joe the Joker, but Rosa.

A Piece of Pie

On Boylston Street, in the city of Boston, Mass., there is a joint where you can get as nice a broiled lobster as anybody ever slaps a lip over, and who is in there one evening partaking of this tidbit but a character by the name of Horse Thief and me.

This Horse Thief is called Horsey for short, and he is not called by this name because he ever steals a horse but because it is the consensus of public opinion from coast to coast that he may steal one if the opportunity presents.

Personally, I consider Horsey a very fine character, because any time he is holding anything he is willing to share his good fortune with one and all, and at this time in Boston he is holding plenty. It is the time we make the race meeting at Suffolk Down, and Horsey gets to going very good, indeed, and in fact he is now a character of means, and is my host against the broiled lobster.

Well, at a table next to us are four or five characters who all seem to be well-dressed, and stout-set, and red-faced, and prosperous-looking, and who all speak with the true Boston accent, which consists of many ah's and very few r's. Characters such as these are familiar to anybody who is ever in Boston very much, and they are bound to be politicians, retired cops, or contractors, because Boston is really quite infested with characters of this nature.

I am paying no attention to them, because they are drinking local ale, and talking loud, and long ago I learn that when a Boston character is engaged in aleing himself up, it is a good idea to let him alone, because the best you can get out of him is maybe a boff on the beezer. But Horsey is in there on the old

Ear-ie, and very much interested in their conversation, and finally I listen myself just to hear what is attracting his attention, when one of the characters speaks as follows:

'Well,' he says, 'I am willing to bet ten thousand dollars that he can outeat anybody in the United States any time.'

Now at this, Horsey gets right up and steps over to the table and bows and smiles in a friendly way on one and all, and says:

'Gentlemen,' he says, 'pardon the intrusion, and excuse me for billing in, but,' he says, 'do I understand you are speaking of a great eater who resides in your fair city?'

Well, these Boston characters all gaze at Horsey in such a hostile manner that I am expecting any one of them to get up and request him to let them miss him, but he keeps on bowing and smiling, and they can see that he is a gentleman, and finally one of them says:

'Yes,' he says, 'we are speaking of a character by the name of Joel Duffle. He is without doubt the greatest eater alive. He just wins a unique wager. He bets a character from Bangor, Me., that he can eat a whole window display of oysters in this very restaurant, and he not only eats all the oysters but he then wishes to wager that he can also eat the shells, but,' he says, 'it seems that the character from Bangor, Me., unfortunately taps out on the first proposition and has nothing with which to bet on the second.'

'Very interesting,' Horsey says. 'Very interesting, if true, but,' he says, 'unless my ears deceive me, I hear one of you state that he is willing to wager ten thousand dollars on this eater of yours against anybody in the United States.'

'Your ears are perfect,' another of the Boston characters says. 'I state it, although,' he says, 'I admit it is a sort of figure of speech. But I state it all right,' he says, 'and never let it be said that a Conway ever pigs it on a betting proposition.'

'Well,' Horsey says, 'I do not have a tenner on me at the moment, but,' he says, 'I have here a thousand dollars to put up as a forfeit that I can produce a character who will outeat your party for ten thousand, and as much more as you care to put up.'

And with this, Horsey outs with a bundle of coarse notes and tosses it on the table, and right away one of the Boston characters, whose name turns out to be Carroll, slaps his hand on the money and says:

'Bet.'

Well, now this is prompt action to be sure, and if there is one thing I admire more than anything else, it is action, and I can see that these are characters of true sporting instincts and I commence wondering where I can raise a few dibs to take a piece of Horsey's proposition, because of course I know that he has nobody in mind to do the eating for his side but Nicely-Nicely Jones.

And knowing Nicely-Nicely Jones, I am prepared to wager all the money I can possibly raise that he can outeat anything that walks on two legs. In fact, I will take a chance on Nicely-Nicely against anything on four legs, except maybe an elephant, and at that he may give the elephant a photo finish.

I do not say that Nicely-Nicely is the greatest eater in all history, but what I do say is he belongs up there as a contender. In fact, Professor D, who is a professor in a college out West before he turns to playing the horses for a livelihood, and who makes a study of history in his time, says he will not be surprised but what Nicely-Nicely figures one-two.

Professor D says we must always remember that Nicely-Nicely eats under the handicaps of modern civilization, which require that an eater use a knife and fork, or anyway a knife, while in the old days eating with the hands was a popular custom and much faster. Professor D says he has no doubt that under the old rules Nicely-Nicely will hang up a record that will endure through the ages, but of course maybe Professor D overlays Nicely-Nicely somewhat.

Well, now that the match is agreed upon, naturally Horsey and the Boston characters begin discussing where it is to take place, and one of the Boston characters suggests a neutral ground, such as New London, Conn., or Providence, R.I., but Horsey holds out for New York, and it seems that Boston characters are always ready to visit New York, so he does not meet with any great opposition on this point.

They all agree on a date four weeks later so as to give the principals plenty of time to get ready, although Horsey and I know that this is really unnecessary as far as Nicely-Nicely is concerned, because one thing about him is he is always in condition to eat.

This Nicely-Nicely Jones is a character who is maybe five feet eight inches tall, and about five feet nine inches wide, and when he is in good shape he will weigh upward of two hundred and eighty-three pounds. He is a horse player by trade, and eating is really just a hobby, but he is undoubtedly a wonderful eater even when he is not hungry.

Well, as soon as Horsey and I return to New York, we hasten to Mindy's restaurant on Broadway and relate the bet Horsey makes in Boston, and right away so many citizens, including Mindy himself, wish to take a piece of the proposition that it is oversubscribed by a large sum in no time.

Then Mindy remarks that he does not see Nicely-Nicely Jones for a month of Sundays, and then everybody present remembers that they do not see Nicely-Nicely around lately, either, and this leads to a discussion of where Nicely-Nicely can be, although up to this moment if nobody sees Nicely-Nicely but once in the next ten years it will be considered sufficient.

Well, Willie the Worrier, who is a bookmaker by trade, is among those present, and he remembers that the last time he looks for Nicely-Nicely hoping to collect a marker of some years' standing, Nicely-Nicely is living at the Rest-Hotel in West Forty-ninth Street, and nothing will do Horsey but I must go with him over to the Rest to make inquiry for Nicely-Nicely, and there we learn that he leaves a forwarding address away up on Morningside Heights in care of somebody by the name of Slocum.

So Horsey calls a short, and away we go to this address, which turns out to be a five-story walk-up apartment, and a card downstairs shows that Slocum lives on the top floor. It takes Horsey and me ten minutes to walk up the five flights as we are by no means accustomed to exercise of this nature, and when we finally reach a door marked Slocum, we are plumb tuckered out, and have to sit down on the top step and rest a while.

Then I ring the bell at this door marked Slocum, and who appears but a tall young Judy with black hair who is without doubt beautiful, but who is so skinny we have to look twice to see her, and when I ask her if she can give me any information about a party named Nicely-Nicely Jones, she says to me like this:

'I guess you mean Quentin,' she says. 'Yes,' she says,'Quentin is here. Come in, gentlemen.'

So we step into an apartment, and as we do so a thin, sickly looking character gets up out of a chair by the window, and in a weak voice says good evening. It is a good evening, at that, so Horsey and I say good evening right back at him, very polite, and then we stand there waiting for Nicely-Nicely to appear, when the beautiful skinny young Judy says:

'Well,' she says, 'this is Mr Quentin Jones.'

Then Horsey and I take another swivel at the thin character, and we can see that it is nobody but Nicely-Nicely, at that, but the way he changes since we last observe him is practically shocking to us both, because he is undoubtedly all shrunk up. In fact, he looks as if he is about half what he is in his prime, and his face is pale and thin, and his eyes are away back in his head, and while we both shake hands with him it is some time before either of us is able to speak. Then Horsey finally says:

'Nicely,' he says, 'can we have a few words with you in private on a very important proposition?'

Well, at this, and before Nicely-Nicely can answer aye, yes, or no, the beautiful skinny young Judy goes out of the room and slams a door behind her, and Nicely-Nicely says:

'My fiancée, Miss Hilda Slocum,' he says. 'She is a wonderful character. We are to be married as soon as I lose twenty pounds more. It will take a couple of weeks longer,' he says.

'My goodness gracious, Nicely,' Horsey says. 'What do you mean lose twenty pounds more? You are practically emaciated now. Are you just out of a sick bed, or what?'

'Why,' Nicely-Nicely says, 'certainly I am not out of a sick bed. I am never healthier in my life. I am on a diet. I lose eighty-three pounds in two months, and am now down to two hundred. I feel great,' he says. 'It is all because of my fiancée, Miss Hilda Slocum. She rescues me from gluttony and obesity, or anyway,' Nicely-Nicely says, 'this is what Miss Hilda Slocum calls it. My, I feel good. I love Miss Hilda Slocum very much,' Nicely-Nicely says. 'It is a case of love at first sight on both sides the day we meet in the subway. I am wedged in one of the turnstile gates, and she kindly pushes on me from behind until I wiggle through. I can see she has a kind heart, so I date her up for a movie that night and propose to her while the newsreel is on. But,' Nicely-Nicely says, 'Hilda tells me at once that she will never marry a fat slob. She says I must put myself in her hands and she will reduce me by scientific methods and then she will become my ever-loving wife, but not before.

'So,' Nicely-Nicely says, 'I come to live here with Miss Hilda Slocum and her mother, so she can supervise my diet. Her mother is thinner than Hilda. And I surely feel great,' Nicely-Nicely says. 'Look,' he says.

And with this, he pulls out the waistband of his pants, and shows enough spare space to hide the War Admiral in, but the effort seems to be a strain on him, and he has to sit down in his chair again.

'My goodness gracious,' Horsey says. 'What do you eat, Nicely?'

'Well,' Nicely-Nicely says, 'I eat anything that does not contain starch, but,' he says, 'of course everything worth eating contains starch, so I really do not eat much of anything whatever. My fiancée, Miss Hilda Slocum, arranges my diet. She is an expert dietician and runs a widely known department in a diet magazine by the name of *Let's Keep House*.'

Then Horsey tells Nicely-Nicely of how he is matched to eat

against this Joel Duffle, of Boston, for a nice side bet, and how he has a forfeit of a thousand dollars already posted for appearance, and how many of Nicely-Nicely's admirers along Broadway are looking to win themselves out of all their troubles by betting on him, and at first Nicely-Nicely listens with great interest, and his eyes are shining like six bits, but then he becomes very sad, and says:

'It is no use, gentlemen,' he says. 'My fiancée, Miss Hilda Slocum, will never hear of me going off my diet even for a little while. Only yesterday I try to talk her into letting me have a little pumpernickel instead of toasted whole wheat bread, and she says if I even think of such a thing again, she will break our engagement. Horsey,' he says, 'do you ever eat toasted whole wheat bread for a month hand running? Toasted?' he says. ·

'No,' Horsey says. 'What I eat is nice, white French bread, and corn muffins, and hot biscuits with gravy on them.'

'Stop,' Nicely-Nicely says. 'You are eating yourself into an early grave, and, furthermore,' he says, 'you are breaking my heart. But,' he says, 'the more I think of my following depending on me in this emergency, the sadder it makes me feel to think I am unable to oblige them. However,' he says, 'let us call Miss Hilda Slocum in on an outside chance and see what her reactions to your proposition are.'

So we call Miss Hilda Slocum in, and Horsey explains our predicament in putting so much faith in Nicely-Nicely only to find him dieting, and Miss Hilda Slocum's reactions are to order Horsey and me out of the joint with instructions never to darken her door again, and when we are a block away we can still hear her voice speaking very firmly to Nicely-Nicely.

Well, personally, I figure this ends the matter, for I can see that Miss Hilda Slocum is a most determined character, indeed, and the chances are it does end it, at that, if Horsey does not happen to get a wonderful break.

He is at Belmont Park one afternoon, and he has a real good thing in a jump race, and when a brisk young character in a hard straw hat and eyeglasses comes along and asks him what he likes, Horsey mentions this good thing, figuring he will move himself in for a few dibs if the good thing connects.

Well, it connects all right, and the brisk young character is very grateful to Horsey for his information, and is giving him plenty of much-obliges, and nothing else, and Horsey is about to mention that they do not accept much-obliges at his hotel, when the brisk young character mentions that he is nobody but Mr McBurgle and that he is the editor of the *Let's Keep House* magazine, and for Horsey to drop in and see him any time he is around his way.

Naturally, Horsey remembers what Nicely-Nicely says about Miss Hilda Slocum working for this *Let's Keep House* magazine, and he relates the story of the eating contest to Mr McBurgle and asks him if he will kindly use his influence with Miss Hilda Slocum to get her to release Nicely-Nicely from his diet long enough for the contest. Then Horsey gives Mr McBurgle a tip on another winner, and Mr McBurgle must use plenty of influence on Miss Hilda Slocum at once, as the next day she calls Horsey up at his hotel before he is out of bed, and speaks to him as follows:

'Of course,' Miss Hilda Slocum says, 'I will never change my attitude about Quentin, but,' she says, 'I can appreciate that he feels very bad about you gentlemen relying on him and having to disappoint you. He feels that he lets you down, which is by no means true, but it weighs upon his mind. It is interfering with his diet.

'Now,' Miss Hilda Slocum says, 'I do not approve of your contest, because,' she says, 'it is placing a premium on gluttony, but I have a friend by the name of Miss Violette Shumberger who may answer your purpose. She is my dearest friend from childhood, but it is only because I love her dearly that this friendship endures. She is extremely fond of eating,' Miss Hilda Slocum says. 'In spite of my pleadings, and my warnings, and my own example, she persists in food. It is disgusting to me but I finally learn that it is no use arguing with her.

'She remains my dearest friend,' Miss Hilda Slocum says,

'though she continues her practice of eating, and I am informed that she is phenomenal in this respect. In fact,' she says, 'Nicely-Nicely tells me to say to you that if Miss Violette Shumberger can perform the eating exploits I relate to him from hearsay she is a lily. Goodbye,' Miss Hilda Slocum says. 'You cannot have Nicely-Nicely.'

Well, nobody cares much about this idea of a stand-in for Nicely-Nicely in such a situation, and especially a Judy that no one ever hears of before, and many citizens are in favour of pulling out of the contest altogether. But Horsey has his thousand-dollar forfeit to think of, and as no one can suggest anyone else, he finally arranges a personal meet with the Judy suggested by Miss Hilda Slocum.

He comes into Mindy's one evening with a female character who is so fat it is necessary to push three tables together to give her room for her lap, and it seems that this character is Miss Violette Shumberger. She weighs maybe two hundred and fifty pounds, but she is by no means an old Judy, and by no means bad-looking. She has a face the size of a town clock and enough chins for a fire escape, but she has a nice smile and pretty teeth, and a laugh that is so hearty it knocks the whipped cream off an order of strawberry shortcake on a table fifty feet away and arouses the indignation of a customer by the name of Goldstein who is about to consume same.

Well, Horsey's idea in bringing her into Mindy's is to get some kind of line on her eating form, and she is clocked by many experts when she starts putting on the hot meat, and it is agreed by one and all that she is by no means a selling-plater. In fact, by the time she gets through, even Mindy admits she has plenty of class, and the upshot of it all is Miss Violette Shumberger is chosen to eat against Joel Duffle.

Maybe you hear something of this great eating contest that comes off in New York one night in the early summer of 1937. Of course eating contests are by no means anything new, and in fact they are quite an old-fashioned pastime in some sections of this country, such as the South and East, but this is the first big public contest of the kind in years, and it creates no little comment along Broadway.

In fact, there is some mention of it in the blats, and it is not a frivolous proposition in any respect, and more dough is wagered on it than any other eating contest in history, with Joel Duffle a 6 to 5 favourite over Miss Violette Shumberger all the way through.

This Joel Duffle comes to New York several days before the contest with the character by the name of Conway, and requests a meet with Miss Violette Shumberger to agree on the final details and who shows up with Miss Violette Shumberger as her coach and adviser but Nicely-Nicely Jones. He is even thinner and more peaked-looking than when Horsey and I see him last, but he says he feels great, and that he is within six pounds of his marriage to Miss Hilda Slocum.

Well, it seems that his presence is really due to Miss Hilda Slocum herself, because she says that after getting her dearest friend Miss Violette Shumberger into this jackpot, it is only fair to do all she can to help her win it, and the only way she can think of is to let Nicely-Nicely give Violette the benefit of his experience and advice.

But afterward we learn that what really happens is that this editor, Mr McBurgle, gets greatly interested in the contest, and when he discovers that in spite of his influence, Miss Hilda Slocum declines to permit Nicely-Nicely to personally compete, but puts in a pinch eater, he is quite indignant and insists on her letting Nicely-Nicely school Violette.

Furthermore we afterward learn that when Nicely-Nicely returns to the apartment on Morningside Heights after giving Violette a lesson, Miss Hilda Slocum always smells his breath to see if he indulges in any food during his absence.

Well, this Joel Duffle is a tall character with stooped shoulders, and a sad expression, and he does not look as if he can eat his way out of a tea shoppe, but as soon as he commences to discuss the details of the contest, anybody can see that he knows what time it is in situations such as this. In fact, Nicely-

Nicely says he can tell at once from the way Joel Duffle talks that he is a dangerous opponent, and he says while Miss Violette Shumberger impresses him as an improving eater, he is only sorry she does not have more seasoning.

This Joel Duffle suggests that the contest consist of twelve courses of strictly American food, each side to be allowed to pick six dishes, doing the picking in rotation, and specifying the weight and quantity of the course selected to any amount the contestant making the pick desires, and each course is to be divided for eating exactly in half, and after Miss Violette Shumberger and Nicely-Nicely whisper together a while, they say the terms are quite satisfactory.

Then Horsey tosses a coin for the first pick, and Joel Duffle says heads, and it is heads, and he chooses, as the first course, two quarts of ripe olives, twelve bunches of celery, and four pounds of shelled nuts, all this to be split fifty-fifty between them. Miss Violette Shumberger names twelve dozen cherry-stone clams as the second course, and Joel Duffle says two gallons of Philadelphia pepper-pot soup as the third.

Well, Miss Violette Shumberger and Nicely-Nicely whisper together again, and Violette puts in two five-pound striped bass, the heads and tails not to count in the eating, and Joel Duffle names a twenty-two pound roast turkey. Each vegetable is rated as one course, and Miss Violette Shumberger asks for twelve pounds of mashed potatoes with brown gravy. Joel Duffle says two dozen ears of corn on the cob, and Violette replies with two quarts of lima beans. Joel Duffle calls for twelve bunches of asparagus cooked in butter, and Violette mentions ten pounds of stewed new peas.

This gets them down to the salad, and it is Joel Duffle's play, so he says six pounds of mixed green salad with vinegar and oil dressing, and now Miss Violette Shumberger has the final selection, which is the dessert. She says it is a pumpkin pie, two feet across, and not less than three inches deep.

It is agreed that they must eat with knife, fork or spoon, but speed is not to count, and there is to be no time limit, except they cannot pause more than two consecutive minutes at any stage, except in case of hiccoughs. They can drink anything, and as much as they please, but liquids are not to count in the scoring. The decision is to be strictly on the amount of food consumed, and the judges are to take account of anything left on the plates after a course, but not of loose chewings on bosom or vest up to an ounce. The losing side is to pay for the food, and in case of a tie they are to eat it off immediately on ham and eggs only.

Well, the scene of this contest is the second-floor dining-room of Mindy's restaurant, which is closed to the general public for the occasion, and only parties immediately concerned in the contest are admitted. The contestants are seated on either side of a big table in the centre of the room, and each contestant has three waiters.

No talking and no rooting from the spectators is permitted, but of course in any eating contest the principals may speak to each other if they wish, though smart eaters never wish to do this, as talking only wastes energy, and about all they ever say to each other is please pass the mustard.

About fifty characters from Boston are present to witness the contest, and the same number of citizens of New York are admitted, and among them is this editor, Mr McBurgle, and he is around asking Horsey if he thinks Miss Violette Shumberger is as good a thing as the jumper at the race track.

Nicely-Nicely arrives on the scene quite early, and his appearance is really most distressing to his old friends and admirers, as by this time he is shy so much weight that he is a pitiful scene, to be sure, but he tells Horsey and me that he thinks Miss Violette Shumberger has a good chance.

'Of course,' he says, 'she is green. She does not know how to pace herself in competition. But,' he says, 'she has a wonderful style. I love to watch her eat. She likes the same things I do in the days when I am eating. She is a wonderful character, too. Do you ever notice her smile?' Nicely-Nicely says.

'But,' he says, 'she is the dearest friend of my fiancée, Miss

Hilda Slocum, so let us not speak of this. I try to get Hilda to come to see the contest, but she says it is repulsive. Well, anyway,' Nicely-Nicely says, 'I manage to borrow a few dibs, and am wagering on Miss Violette Shumberger. By the way,' he says, 'if you happen to think of it, notice her smile.'

Well, Nicely-Nicely takes a chair about ten feet behind Miss Violette Shumberger, which is as close as the judges will allow him, and he is warned by them that no coaching from the corners will be permitted, but of course Nicely-Nicely knows this rule as well as they do, and furthermore by this time his exertions seem to have left him without any more energy.

There are three judges, and they are all from neutral territory. One of these judges is a party from Baltimore, Md., by the name of Packard, who runs a restaurant, and another is a party from Providence, R.I., by the name of Croppers, who is a sausage manufacturer. The third judge is an old Judy by the name of Mrs Rhubarb, who comes from Philadelphia, and once keeps an actors' boarding-house, and is considered an excellent judge of eaters.

Well, Mindy is the official starter, and at 8.30 p.m. sharp, when there is still much betting among the spectators, he outs with his watch, and says like this:

'Are you ready, Boston? Are you ready, New York?'

Miss Violette Shumberger and Joel Duffle both nod their heads, and Mindy says commence, and the contest is on, with Joel Duffle getting the jump at once on the celery and olives and nuts.

It is apparent that this Joel Duffle is one of these rough-and-tumble eaters that you can hear quite a distance off, especially on clams and soups. He is also an eyebrow eater, an eater whose eyebrows go up as high as the part in his hair as he eats, and this type of eater is undoubtedly very efficient.

In fact, the way Joel Duffle goes through the groceries down to the turkey causes the Broadway spectators some uneasiness, and they are whispering to each other that they only wish the old Nicely-Nicely is in there. But personally, I like the way

Miss Violette Shumberger eats without undue excitement, and with great zest. She cannot keep close to Joel Duffle in the matter of speed in the early stages of the contest, as she seems to enjoy chewing her food, but I observe that as it goes along she pulls up on him, and I figure this is not because she is stepping up her pace, but because he is slowing down.

When the turkey finally comes on, and is split in two halves right down the middle, Miss Violette Shumberger looks greatly disappointed, and she speaks for the first time as follows:

'Why,' she says, 'where is the stuffing?'

Well, it seems that nobody mentions any stuffing for the turkey to the chef, so he does not make any stuffing, and Miss Violette Shumberger's disappointment is so plain to be seen that the confidence of the Boston characters is somewhat shaken. They can see that a Judy who can pack away as much fodder as Miss Violette Shumberger has to date, and then beef for stuffing, is really quite an eater.

In fact, Joel Duffle looks quite startled when he observes Miss Violette Shumberger's disappointment, and he gazes at her with great respect as she disposes of her share of the turkey, and the mashed potatoes, and one thing and another in such a manner that she moves up on the pumpkin pie on dead even terms with him. In fact, there is little to choose between them at this point, although the judge from Baltimore is calling the attention of the other judges to a turkey leg that he claims Miss Violette Shumberger does not clean as neatly as Joel Duffle does his, but the other judges dismiss this as a technicality.

Then the waiters bring on the pumpkin pie, and it is without doubt quite a large pie, and in fact it is about the size of a manhole cover, and I can see that Joel Duffle is observing this pie with a strange expression on his face, although to tell the truth I do not care for the expression on Miss Violette Shumberger's face, either.

Well, the pie is cut in two dead centre, and one half is placed before Miss Violette Shumberger and the other half before Joel

Duffle, and he does not take more than two bites before I see him loosen his waistband and take a big swig of water, and thinks I to myself, he is now down to a slow walk, and the pie will decide the whole heat, and I am only wishing I am able to wager a little more dough on Miss Violette Shumberger. But about this moment, and before she as much as touches her pie, all of a sudden Violette turns her head and motions to Nicely-Nicely to approach her, and as he approaches, she whispers in his ear.

Now at this, the Boston character by the name of Conway jumps up and claims a foul and several other Boston characters join him in this claim, and so does Joel Duffle, although afterwards even the Boston characters admit that Joel Duffle is no gentleman to make such a claim against a lady.

Well, there is some confusion over this, and the judges hold a conference, and they rule that there is certainly no foul in the actual eating that they can see, because Miss Violette Shumberger does not touch her pie so far.

But they say that whether it is a foul otherwise all depends on whether Miss Violette Shumberger is requesting advice on the contest from Nicely-Nicely and the judge from Providence, R.I., wishes to know if Nicely-Nicely will kindly relate what passes between him and Violette so they may make a decision.

'Why,' Nicely-Nicely says, 'all she asks me is can I get her another piece of pie when she finishes the one in front of her.'

Now at this, Joel Duffle throws down his knife, and pushes back his plate with all but two bites of his pie left on it, and says to the Boston characters like this:

'Gentlemen,' he says, 'I am licked. I cannot eat another mouthful. You must admit I put up a game battle, but,' he says, 'it is useless for me to go on against this Judy who is asking for more pie before she even starts on what is before her. I am almost dying as it is, and I do not wish to destroy myself in a hopeless effort. Gentlemen,' he says, 'she is not human.'

Well, of course this amounts to throwing in the old napkin and Nicely-Nicely stands up on his chair, and says:

'Three cheers for Miss Violette Shumberger!'

Then Nicely-Nicely gives the first cheer in person, but the effort overtaxes his strength, and he falls off the chair in a faint just as Joel Duffle collapses under the table, and the doctors at the Clinic Hospital are greatly baffled to receive, from the same address at the same time, one patient who is suffering from undernourishment, and another patient who is unconscious from overeating.

Well, in the meantime, after the excitement subsides, and wagers are settled, we take Miss Violette Shumberger to the main floor in Mindy's for a midnight snack, and when she speaks of her wonderful triumph, she is disposed to give much credit to Nicely-Nicely Jones.

'You see,' Violette says, 'what I really whisper to him is that I am a goner. I whisper to him that I cannot possibly take one bite of the pie if my life depends on it, and if he has any bets down to try and hedge them off as quickly as possible.

'I fear,' she says, 'that Nicely-Nicely will be greatly disappointed in my showing, but I have a confession to make to him when he gets out of the hospital. I forget about the contest,' Violette says, 'and eat my regular dinner of pig's knuckles and sauerkraut an hour before the contest starts and,' she says, 'I have no doubt this tends to affect my form somewhat. So,' she says, 'I owe everything to Nicely-Nicely's quick thinking.'

It is several weeks after the great eating contest that I run into Miss Hilda Slocum on Broadway and it seems to me that she looks much better nourished than the last time I see her, and when I mention this she says:

'Yes,' she says, 'I cease dieting. I learn my lesson,' she says. 'I learn that male characters do not appreciate anybody who tries to ward off surplus tissue. What male characters wish is substance. Why,' she says, 'only a week ago my editor, Mr McBurgle, tells me he will love to take me dancing if only I get something on me for him to take hold of. I am very fond of dancing,' she says.

'But,' I say, 'what of Nicely-Nicely Jones? I do not see him around lately.'

'Why,' Miss Hilda Slocum says, 'do you not hear what this cad does? Why, as soon as he is strong enough to leave the hospital, he elopes with my dearest friend, Miss Violette Shumberger, leaving me a note saying something about two souls with but a single thought. They are down in Florida running a barbecue stand, and,' she says, 'the chances are, eating like seven mules.'

'Miss Slocum,' I say, 'can I interest you in a portion of Mindy's chicken fricassee?'

'With dumplings?' Miss Hilda Slocum says. 'Yes,' she says, 'you can. Afterwards I have a date to go dancing with Mr McBurgle. I am crazy about dancing,' she says.

Johnny One-Eye

This cat I am going to tell you about is a very small cat, and in fact it is only a few weeks old, consequently it is really nothing but an infant cat. To tell the truth, it is just a kitten.

It is grey and white and very dirty and its fur is all frowzled up, so it is a very miserable-looking little kitten to be sure the day it crawls through a broken basement window into an old house in East Fifty-third Street over near Third Avenue in the city of New York and goes from room to room saying merouw, merouw in a low, weak voice until it comes to a room at the head of the stairs on the second storey where a guy by the name of Rudolph is sitting on the floor thinking of not much.

One reason Rudolph is sitting on the floor is because there is nothing else to sit on as this is an empty house that is all boarded up for years and there is no furniture whatever in it, and another reason is that Rudolph has a .38 slug in his side and really does not feel like doing much of anything but sitting. He is wearing a derby hat and his overcoat as it is in the wintertime and very cold and he has an automatic Betsy on the floor beside him and naturally he is surprised quite some when the little kitten comes merouwing into the room and he picks up the Betsy and points it at the door in case anyone he does not wish to see is with the kitten. But when he observes that it is all alone, Rudolph puts the Betsy down again and speaks to the kitten as follows:

'Hello, cat,' he says.

Of course the kitten does not say anything in reply except merouw but it walks right up to Rudolph and climbs on his lap, although the chances are if it knows who Rudolph is it will hightail it out of there quicker than anybody can say scat.

There is enough daylight coming through the chinks in the boards over the windows for Rudolph to see that the kitten's right eye is in bad shape, and in fact it is bulged half out of its head in a most distressing manner and it is plain to be seen that the sight is gone from this eye. It is also plain to be seen that the injury happened recently and Rudolph gazes at the kitten a while and starts to laugh and says like this:

'Well, cat,' he says, 'you seem to be scuffed up almost as much as I am. We make a fine pair of invalids here together. What is your name, cat?'

Naturally the kitten does not state its name but only goes merouw and Rudolph says, 'All right, I will call you Johnny. Yes,' he says, 'your tag is now Johnny One-Eye.'

Then he puts the kitten in under his overcoat and pretty soon it gets warm and starts to purr and Rudolph says:

'Johnny,' he says, 'I will say one thing for you and that is you are plenty game to be able to sing when you are hurt as bad as you are. It is more than I can do.'

But Johnny only goes merouw again and keeps on purring and by and by it falls sound asleep under Rudolph's coat and Rudolph is wishing the pain in his side will let up long enough for him to do the same.

Well, I suppose you are saying to yourself, what is this Rudolph doing in an old empty house with a slug in his side, so I will explain that the district attorney is responsible for this situation. It seems that the D.A. appears before the grand jury and tells it that Rudolph is an extortion guy and a killer and I do not know what all else, though some of these statements are without doubt a great injustice to Rudolph as, up to the time the D.A. makes them, Rudolph does not kill anybody of any consequence in years.

It is true that at one period of his life he is considered a little wild but this is in the 1920's when everybody else is, too, and for seven or eight years he is all settled down and is engaged in business organization work, which is very respectable work, indeed. He organizes quite a number of businesses on a large scale and is doing very good for himself. He is living quietly in a big hotel all alone, as Rudolph is by no means a family guy, and he is highly spoken of by one and all when the D.A. starts poking his nose into his affairs, claiming that Rudolph has no right to be making money out of the businesses, even though Rudolph gives these businesses plenty of first-class protection.

In fact, the D.A. claims that Rudolph is nothing but a racket guy and a great knock to the community, and all this upsets Rudolph no little when it comes to his ears in a roundabout way.

So he calls up his lawbooks and requests legal advice on the subject and lawbooks says the best thing he can think of for Rudolph to do is to become as inconspicuous as possible right away but to please not mention to anyone that he gives this advice.

Lawbooks says he understands the D.A. is requesting indictments and is likely to get them and furthermore that he is rounding up certain parties that Rudolph is once associated with and trying to get them to remember incidents in Rudolph's early career that may not be entirely to his credit. Lawbooks says he hears that one of these parties is a guy by the name of Cute Freddy and that Freddy makes a deal with the D.A. to lay off him if he tells everything he knows about Rudolph, so under the circumstances a long journey by Rudolph will be in the interest of everybody concerned.

So Rudolph decides to go on a journey but then he gets to thinking that maybe Freddy will remember a little matter that Rudolph long ago since dismisses from his mind and does not wish to have recalled again, which is the time he and Freddy do a job on a guy by the name of The Icelander in Troy years ago and he drops around to Freddy's house to remind him to be sure not to remember this.

But it seems that Freddy, who is an important guy in business organization work himself, though in a different part of the city than Rudolph, mistakes the purpose of Rudolph's visit and starts to out with his rooty-toot-toot and in order to protect himself it is necessary for Rudolph to take his Betsy and give Freddy a little tattooing. In fact, Rudolph practically crockets his monogram on Freddy's chest and leaves him exceptionally deceased.

But as Rudolph is departing from the neighbourhood, who bobs up but a young guy by the name of Buttsy Fagan, who works for Freddy as a chauffeur and one thing and another, and who is also said to be able to put a slug through a keyhole at forty paces without touching the sides though I suppose it will have to be a pretty good-sized keyhole. Anyway, he takes a long-distance crack at Rudolph as Rudolph is rounding a corner, but all Buttsy can see of Rudolph at the moment is a little piece of his left side and this is what Buttsy hits, although no one knows it at the time, except of course Rudolph, who just keeps on departing.

Now this incident causes quite a stir in police circles, and the D.A. is very indignant over losing a valuable witness and when they are unable to locate Rudolph at once, a reward of five thousand dollars is offered for information leading to his capture alive or dead and some think they really mean dead. Indeed, it is publicly stated that it is not a good idea for anyone to take any chances with Rudolph as he is known to be armed and is such a character as will be sure to resent being captured, but they do not explain that this is only because Rudolph knows the D.A. wishes to place him in the old rocking-chair at Sing Sing and that Rudolph is quite allergic to the idea.

Anyway, the cops go looking for Rudolph in Hot Springs and Miami and every other place except where he is, which is right in New York wandering around town with the slug in his side, knocking at the doors of old friends requesting assistance. But all the old friends do for him is to slam the doors in his face and forget they ever see him, as the D.A. is very tough on parties who assists guys he is looking for, claiming that this is something most illegal called harbouring fugitives. Besides Rudolph is never any too popular at best with his old friends as he always plays pretty much of a lone duke and takes the big end of everything for his.

He cannot even consult a doctor about the slug in his side as he knows that nowadays the first thing a doctor will do about a guy with a gunshot wound is to report him to the cops, although Rudolph can remember when there is always a sure-footed doctor around who will consider it a privilege and a pleasure to treat him and keep his trap closed about it. But of course this is in the good old days and Rudolph can see they are gone forever. So he just does the best he can about the slug and goes on wandering here and there and around and about and the blats keep printing his picture and saying, where is Rudolph?

Where he is some of the time is in Central Park trying to get some sleep, but of course even the blats will consider it foolish to go looking for Rudolph there in such cold weather, as he is a guy who enjoys his comfort at all times. In fact, it is comfort that Rudolph misses more than anything as the slug is commencing to cause him great pain and naturally the pain turns Rudolph's thoughts to the author of same and he remembers that he once hears somebody say that Buttsy lives over in East Fifty-third Street.

So one night Rudolph decides to look Buttsy up and cause him a little pain in return and he is moseying through Fifty-third when he gets so weak he falls down on the sidewalk in front of the old house and rolls down a short flight of steps that lead from the street level to a little railed-in area-way and ground floor or basement door and before he stops rolling he brings up against the door itself and it creaks open inward as he bumps it. After he lays there awhile Rudolph can see that the house is empty and he crawls on inside.

Then when he feels stronger, Rudolph makes his way upstairs because the basement is damp and mice keep trotting back and forth over him and eventually he winds up in the room where Johnny One-Eye finds him the following afternoon and the reason Rudolph settles down in this room is because it commands the stairs. Naturally, this is important to a guy in Rudolph's situation, though after he is sitting there for about

fourteen hours before Johnny comes along he can see that he is
not going to be much disturbed by traffic. But he considers it a
very fine place, indeed, to remain planted until he is able to
resume his search for Buttsy.

Well, after a while Johnny One-Eye wakes up and comes
from under the coat and looks at Rudolph out of his good eye
and Rudolph waggles his fingers and Johnny plays with them,
catching one finger in his front paws and biting it gently and
this pleases Rudolph no little as he never before has any
personal experience with a kitten. However, he remembers
observing one when he is a boy down in Houston Street, so he
takes a piece of paper out of his pocket and makes a little ball of
it and rolls it along the floor and Johnny bounces after it very
lively indeed. But Rudolph can see that the bad eye is getting
worse and finally he says to Johnny like this:

'Johnny,' he says, 'I guess you must be suffering more than I
am. I remember there are some pet shops over on Lexington
Avenue not far from here and when it gets good and dark I am
going to take you out and see if we can find a cat croaker to do
something about your eye. Yes, Johnny,' Rudolph says, 'I will
also get you something to eat. You must be starved.'

Johnny One-Eye says merouw to this and keeps on playing
with the paper ball but soon it comes on dark outside and
inside too, and, in fact, it is so dark inside that Rudolph cannot
see his hand before him. Then he puts his Betsy in a side
pocket of his overcoat and picks up Johnny and goes downstairs,
feeling his way in the dark and easing along a step at a time
until he gets to the basement door. Naturally, Rudolph does
not wish to strike any matches because he is afraid someone
outside may see the light and get nosey.

By moving very slowly, Rudolph finally gets to Lexington
Avenue and while he is going along he remembers the time he
walks from 125th Street in Harlem down to 110th with six
slugs in him and never feels as bad as he does now. He gets to
thinking that maybe he is not the guy he used to be, which of
course is very true as Rudolph is now forty-odd years of age

and is fat around the middle and getting bald, and he also does some thinking about what a pleasure it will be to him to find this Buttsy and cause him the pain he is personally suffering.

There are not many people in the streets and those that are go hurrying along because it is so cold and none of them pay any attention to Rudolph or Johnny One-Eye either, even though Rudolph staggers a little now and then like a guy who is rummed up, although of course it is only weakness. The chances are he is also getting a little feverish and lightheaded because finally he stops a cop who is going along swinging his arms to keep warm and asks him if he knows where there is a pet shop and it is really most indiscreet of such a guy as Rudolph to be interviewing cops. But the cop just points up the street and goes on without looking twice at Rudolph and Rudolph laughs and pokes Johnny with a finger and says:

'No, Johnny One-Eye,' he says, 'the cop is not a dope for not recognizing Rudolph. Who can figure the hottest guy in forty-eight states to be going along a street with a little cat in his arms? Can you, Johnny?'

Johnny says merouw and pretty soon Rudolph comes to the pet shop the cop points out. Rudolph goes inside and says to the guy like this:

'Are you a cat croaker?' Rudolph says. 'Do you know what to do about a little cat that has a hurt eye?'

'I am a kind of a vet,' the guy says.

'Then take a glaum at Johnny One-Eye here and see what you can do for him,' Rudolph says.

Then he hands Johnny over to the guy and the guy looks at Johnny a while and says:

'Mister,' he says, 'the best thing I can do for this cat is to put it out of its misery. You better let me give it something right now. It will just go to sleep and never know what happens.'

Well, at this, Rudolph grabs Johnny One-Eye out of the guy's hands and puts him under his coat and drops a duke on the Betsy in his pocket as if he is afraid the guy will take Johnny away from him again and he says to the guy like this:

'No, no, no,' Rudolph says. 'I cannot bear to think of such a thing. What about some kind of an operation? I remember they take a bum lamp out of Joe the Goat at Bellevue one time and he is okay now.'

'Nothing will do your cat any good,' the guy says. 'It is a goner. It will start having fits pretty soon and die sure. What is the idea of trying to save such a cat as this? It is no kind of a cat to begin with. It is just a cat. You can get a million like it for a nickel.'

'No,' Rudolph says, 'this is not just a cat. This is Johnny One-Eye. He is my only friend in the world. He is the only living thing that ever comes pushing up against me warm and friendly and trusts me in my whole life. I feel sorry for him.'

'I feel sorry for him, too,' the guy says. 'I always feel sorry for animals that get hurt and for people.'

'I do not feel sorry for people,' Rudolph says. 'I only feel sorry for Johnny One-Eye. Give me some kind of stuff that Johnny will eat.'

'Your cat wants milk,' the guy says. 'You can get some at the delicatessen store down at the corner. Mister,' he says, 'you look sick yourself. Can I do anything for you?'

But Rudolph only shakes his head and goes on out and down to the delicatessen joint where he buys a bottle of milk and this transaction reminds him that he is very short in the moo department. In fact, he can find only a five-dollar note in his pockets and he remembers that he has no way of getting any more when this runs out, which is a very sad predicament indeed for a guy who is accustomed to plenty of moo at all times.

Then Rudolph returns to the old house and sits down on the floor again and gives Johnny One-Eye some of the milk in his derby hat as he neglects buying something for Johnny to drink out of. But Johnny offers no complaint. He laps up the milk and curls himself into a wad in Rudolph's lap and purrs.

Rudolph takes a swig of the milk himself but it makes him sick for by this time Rudolph is really far from being in the pink of condition. He not only has the pain in his side but he has a heavy cold which he probably catches from lying on the basement floor or maybe sleeping in the park and he is wheezing no little. He commences to worry that he may get too ill to continue looking for Buttsy, as he can see that if it is not for Buttsy he will not be in this situation, suffering the way he is, but on a long journey to some place.

He takes to going off into long stretches of a kind of stupor and every time he comes out of one of these stupors the first thing he does is to look around for Johnny One-Eye and Johnny is always right there either playing with the paper ball or purring in Rudolph's lap. He is a great comfort to Rudolph but after a while Rudolph notices that Johnny seems to be running out of zip and he also notices that he is running out of zip himself especially when he discovers that he is no longer able to get to his feet.

It is along in the late afternoon of the day following the night Rudolph goes out of the house that he hears someone coming up the stairs and naturally he picks up his Betsy and gets ready for action when he also hears a very small voice calling kitty, kitty, kitty, and he realizes that the party that is coming can be nobody but a child. In fact, a minute later a little pretty of maybe six years of age comes into the room all out of breath and says to Rudolph like this:

'How do you do?' she says. 'Have you seen my kitty?'

Then she spots Johnny One-Eye in Rudolph's lap and runs over and sits down beside Rudolph and takes Johnny in her arms and at first Rudolph is inclined to resent this and has a notion to give her a good boffing but he is too weak to exert himself in such a manner.

'Who are you?' Rudolph says to the little pretty, 'and,' he says, 'where do you live and how do you get in this house?'

'Why,' she says, 'I am Elsie, and I live down the street and I am looking everywhere for my kitty for three days and the door is open downstairs and I know kitty likes to go in doors that are open so I came to find her and here she is.'

'I guess I forgot to close it last night,' Rudolph says. 'I seem to be very forgetful lately.'

'What is your name?' Elsie asks, 'and why are you sitting on the floor in the cold and where are all your chairs? Do you have any little girls like me and do you love them dearly?'

'No,' Rudolph says. 'By no means and not at all.'

'Well,' Elsie says, 'I think you are a nice man for taking care of my kitty. Do you love kitty?'

'Look,' Rudolph says, 'his name is not kitty. His name is Johnny One-Eye, because he has only one eye.'

'I call her kitty,' Elsie says. 'But,' she says, 'Johnny One-Eye is a nice name too and if you like it best I will call her Johnny and I will leave her here with you to take care of always and I will come to see her every day. You see,' she says, 'if I take Johnny home Buttsy will only kick her again.'

'Buttsy?' Rudolph says. 'Do I hear you say Buttsy? Is his other name Fagan?'

'Why, yes,' Elsie says. 'Do you know him?'

'No,' Rudolph says, 'but I hear of him. What is he to you?'

'He is my new daddy,' Elsie says. 'My other one and my best one is dead and so my mamma makes Buttsy my new one. My mamma says Buttsy is her mistake. He is very mean. He kicks Johnny and hurts her eye and makes her run away. He kicks my mamma too. Buttsy kicks everybody and everything when he is mad and he is always mad.'

'He is a louse to kick a little cat,' Rudolph says.

'Yes,' Elsie says, 'that is what Mr O'Toole says he is for kicking my mamma but my mamma says it is not a nice word and I am never to say it out loud.'

'Who is Mr O'Toole?' Rudolph says.

'He is the policeman,' Elsie says. 'He lives across the street from us and he is very nice to me. He says Buttsy is the word you say just now, not only for kicking my mamma but for taking her money when she brings it home from work and spending it so she cannot buy me nice things to wear. But do you know what?' Elsie says. 'My mamma says some day Buttsy is going far away and then she will buy me lots of things and send me to school and make me a lady.'

Then Elsie begins skipping around the room with Johnny One-Eye in her arms and singing I am going to be a lady, I am going to be a lady, until Rudolph has to tell her to pipe down because he is afraid somebody may hear her. And all the time Rudolph is thinking of Buttsy and regretting that he is unable to get on his pins and go out of the house.

'Now I must go home,' Elsie says, 'because this is a night Buttsy comes in for his supper and I have to be in bed before he gets there so I will not bother him. Buttsy does not like little girls. Buttsy does not like little kittens, Buttsy does not like little anythings. My mamma is afraid of Buttsy and so am I. But,' she says, 'I will leave Johnny here with you and come back tomorrow to see her.'

'Listen, Elsie,' Rudolph says, 'does Mr O'Toole come home tonight to his house for his supper, too?'

'Oh, yes,' Elsie says. 'He comes home every night. Sometimes when there is a night Buttsy is not coming in for his supper my mamma lets me go over to Mr O'Toole's and I play with his dog Charley but you must never tell Buttsy this because he does not like O'Toole either. But this is a night Buttsy is coming and that is why my mamma tells me to get in early.'

Now Rudolph takes an old letter out of his inside pocket and a pencil out of another pocket and he scribbles a few lines on the envelope and stretches himself out on the floor and begins groaning, oh, oh, oh, and then he says to Elsie like this:

'Look, Elsie,' he says, 'you are a smart little kid and you pay strict attention to what I am going to say to you. Do not go to bed tonight until Buttsy gets in. Then,' Rudolph says, 'you tell him you come in this old house looking for your cat and that you hear somebody groaning like I do just now in the room at the head of the stairs and that you find a guy who says his name is Rudolph lying on the floor so sick he cannot move. Tell him the front door of the basement is open. But,' Rudolph says, 'you must not tell him that Rudolph tells you to say these things. Do you understand?'

'Oh,' Elsie says, 'do you want him to come here? He will kick Johnny again if he does.'

'He will come here, but he will not kick Johnny,' Rudolph says. 'He will come here, or I am the worst guesser in the world. Tell him what I look like, Elsie. Maybe he will ask you if you see a gun. Tell him you do not see one. You do not see a gun, do you, Elsie?'

'No,' Elsie says, 'only the one in your hand when I come in but you put it under your coat. Buttsy has a gun and Mr O'Toole has a gun but Buttsy says I am never, never to tell anybody about this or he will kick me the way he does my mamma.'

'Well,' Rudolph says, 'you must not remember seeing mine, either. It is a secret between you and me and Johnny One-Eye. Now,' he says, 'if Buttsy leaves the house to come and see me, as I am pretty sure he will, you run over to Mr O'Toole's house and give him this note, but do not tell Buttsy or your mamma either about the note. If Buttsy does not leave, it is my hard luck, but you give the note to Mr O'Toole anyway. Now tell me what you are to do, Elsie,' Rudolph says, 'so I can see if you have got everything correct.'

'I am to go on home and wait for Buttsy,' she says, 'and I am to tell him Rudolph is lying on the floor of this dirty old house with a fat stomach and a big nose making noises and that he is very sick and the basement door is open and there is no gun if he asks me, and when Buttsy comes to see you I am to take this note to Mr O'Toole but Buttsy and my mamma are not to know I have the note and if Buttsy does not leave I am to give it to Mr O'Toole anyway and you are to stay here and take care of Johnny my kitten.'

'That is swell,' Rudolph says. 'Now you run along.'

So Elsie leaves and Rudolph sits up again against the wall because his side feels easier this way and Johnny One-Eye is in his lap purring very low and the dark comes on until it is blacker inside the room than in the middle of a tunnel and Rudolph feels that he is going into another stupor and he has a tough time fighting it off.

Afterwards some of the neighbours claim they remember hearing a shot inside the house and then two more in quick succession and then all is quiet until a little later when Officer O'Toole and half a dozen other cops and an ambulance with a doctor come busting into the street and swarm into the joint with their guns out and their flashlights going. The first thing they find is Buttsy at the foot of the stairs with two bullet wounds close together in his throat, and naturally he is real dead.

Rudolph is still sitting against the wall with what seems to be a small bundle of bloody fur in his lap but which turns out to be what is left of this little cat I am telling you about, although nobody pays any attention to it at first. They are more interested in getting the come-alongs on Rudolph's wrists but before they move him he pulls his clothes aside and shows the doctor where the slug is in his side and the doctor takes one glaum and shakes his head and says:

'Gangrene,' he says. 'I think you have pneumonia, too, from the way you are blowing.'

'I know,' Rudolph says. 'I know this morning. Not much chance, hey, croaker?'

'Not much,' the doctor says.

'Well, cops,' Rudolph says, 'load me in. I do not suppose you want Johnny, seeing that he is dead.'

'Johnny who?' one of the cops says.

'Johnny One-Eye,' Rudolph says. 'This little cat here in my lap. Buttsy shoots Johnny's only good eye out and takes most of his noodle with it. I never see a more wonderful shot. Well, Johnny is better off but I feel sorry about him as he is my best friend down to the last.'

Then he begins to laugh and the cop asks him what tickles him so much and Rudolph says:

'Oh,' he says, 'I am thinking of the joke on Buttsy. I am

positive he will come looking for me, all right, not only because of the little altercation between Cute Freddy and me but because the chances are Buttsy is greatly embarrassed by not tilting me over the first time, as of course he never knows he wings me. Furthermore,' Rudolph says, 'and this is the best reason of all, Buttsy will realize that if I am in his neighbourhood it is by no means a good sign for him, even if he hears I am sick.

'Well,' Rudolph says, 'I figure that with any kind of a square rattle I will have a better chance of nailing him than he has of nailing me, but that even if he happens to nail me, O'Toole will get my note in time to arrive here and nab Buttsy on the spot with his gun on him. And,' Rudolph says, 'I know it will be a great pleasure to the D.A. to settle Buttsy for having a gun on him.

'But,' Rudolph says, 'as soon as I hear Buttsy coming on the sneaksby up the stairs, I can see I am taking all the worst of it because I am now wheezing like a busted valve and you can hear me a block away except when I hold my breath, which is very difficult indeed, considering the way I am already greatly tuckered out. No,' Rudolph says, 'it does not look any too good for me as Buttsy keeps coming up the stairs, as I can tell he is doing by a little faint creak in the boards now and then. I am in no shape to manœuvre around the room and pretty soon he will be on the landing and then all he will have to do is to wait there until he hears me which he is bound to do unless I stop breathing altogether. Naturally,' Rudolph says, 'I do not care to risk a blast in the dark without knowing where he is as something tells me Buttsy is not a guy you can miss in safety.

'Well,' Rudolph says, 'I notice several times before this that in the dark Johnny One-Eye's good glim shines like a big spark, so when I feel Buttsy is about to hit the landing, although of course I cannot see him, I flip Johnny's ball of paper across the room to the wall just opposite the door and tough as he must be feeling Johnny chases after it when he hears it light. I figure Buttsy will hear Johnny playing with the paper and see his eye shining and think it is me and take a pop at it and that his gun flash will give me a crack at him.

'It all works out just like I dope it,' Rudolph says, 'but,' he says, 'I never give Buttsy credit for being such a marksman as to be able to hit a cat's eye in the dark. If I know this, maybe I will never stick Johnny out in front the way I do. It is a good thing I never give Buttsy a second shot. He is a lily. Yes,' Rudolph says, 'I can remember when I can use a guy like him.'

'Buttsy is no account,' the cop says. 'He is a good riddance. He is the makings of a worse guy than you.'

'Well,' Rudolph says, 'it is a good lesson to him for kicking a little cat.'

Then they take Rudolph to a hospital and this is where I see him and piece out this story of Johnny One-Eye, and Officer O'Toole is at Rudolph's bedside keeping guard over him, and I remember that not long before Rudolph chalks out he looks at O'Toole and says to him like this:

'Copper,' he says, 'there is no chance of them out-juggling the kid on the reward moo, is there?'

'No,' O'Toole says, 'no chance. I keep the note you send me by Elsie saying she will tell me where you are. It is information leading to your capture just as the reward offer states. Rudolph,' he says, 'it is a nice thing you do for Elsie and her mother, although,' he says, 'it is not nearly as nice as icing Buttsy for them.'

'By the way, copper,' Rudolph says, 'there is the remainders of a pound note in my pants pocket when I am brought here. I want you to do me a favour. Get it from the desk and buy Elsie another cat and name it Johnny, will you?'

'Sure,' O'Toole says. 'Anything else?'

'Yes,' Rudolph says, 'be sure it has two good eyes.'

The Brain Goes Home

One night The Brain is walking me up and down Broadway in front of Mindy's restaurant, and speaking of this and that, when along comes a red-headed raggedy doll selling apples at five cents per copy, and The Brain, being very fond of apples, grabs one out of her basket and hands her a five-dollar bill.

The red-headed raggedy doll, who is maybe thirty-odd and is nothing but a crow as far as looks are concerned, squints at the finnif, and says to The Brain like this:

'I do not have change for so much money,' she says, 'but I will go and get it in a minute.'

'You keep the change,' The Brain says, biting a big hunk out of the apple and taking my arm to start me walking again.

Well, the raggedy doll looks at The Brain again, and it seems to me that all of a sudden there are large tears in her eyes as she says:

'Oh, thank you, sir! Thank you, thank you, and God bless you, sir!'

And then she goes on up the street in a hurry, with her hands over her eyes and her shoulders shaking, and The Brain turns around very much astonished, and watches her until she is out of sight.

'Why, my goodness!' The Brain says. 'I give Doris Clare ten G's last night, and she does not make half as much fuss over it as this doll does over a pound note.'

'Well,' I say, 'maybe the apple doll needs a pound note more than Doris needs ten G's.'

'Maybe so,' The Brain says. 'And of course, Doris gives me much more in return than just an apple and a God bless me. Doris gives me her love. I guess,' The Brain says, 'that love costs me about as much dough as any guy that ever lives.'

'I guess it does,' I say, and the chances are we both guess right, because off-hand I figure that if The Brain gets out on three hundred G's per year for love, he is running his love business very economically indeed, because it is well known to one and all that The Brain has three different dolls, besides an ever-loving wife.

In fact, The Brain is sometimes spoken of by many citizens as the 'Love King', but only behind his back, because The Brain likes to think his love affairs are a great secret to all but maybe a few, although the only guy I ever see in this town who does not know all about them is a guy who is deaf, dumb, and blind.

I once read a story about a guy by the name of King Solomon who lives a long time ago and who has a thousand dolls all at once, which is going in for dolls on a very large scale indeed, but I guarantee that all of King Solomon's dolls put together are not as expensive as any one of The Brain's dolls. The overhead on Doris Clare alone will drive an ordinary guy daffy, and Doris is practically frugal compared to Cynthia Harris and Bobby Baker.

Then there is Charlotte, who is The Brain's ever-loving wife and who has a society bug and needs plenty of coconuts at all times to keep her a going concern. I once hear The Brain tell Bobby Baker that his ever-loving wife is a bit of an invalid, but as a matter of fact there is never anything the matter with Charlotte that a few bobs will not cure, although of course this goes for nearly every doll in this world who is an invalid.

When a guy is knocking around Broadway as long as The Brain, he is bound to accumulate dolls here and there, but most guys accumulate one at a time, and when this one runs out on him, as Broadway dolls will do, he accumulates another, and so on, and so on, until he is too old to care about such matters as dolls, which is when he is maybe a hundred and four years old, although I hear of several guys who beat even this record.

But when The Brain accumulates a doll he seems to keep her accumulated, and none of them ever run out on him, and while this will be a very great nuisance to the average guy, it pleases The Brain no little because it makes him think he has a very great power over dolls.

'They are not to blame if they fall in love with me,' The Brain says to me one night. 'I will not cause one of them any sorrow for all the world.'

Well, of course, it is most astonishing to me to hear a guy as smart as The Brain using such language, but I figure he may really believe it, because The Brain thinks very good of himself at all times. However, some guys claim that the real reason The Brain keeps all his dolls is because he is too selfish to give them away, although personally I will not take any of them if The Brain throws in a cash bonus, except maybe Bobby Baker.

Anyway, The Brain keeps his dolls accumulated, and furthermore he spends plenty of dough on them, what with buying them automobiles and furs and diamonds and swell places to live in – especially swell places to live in. One time I tell The Brain he will save himself plenty if he hires a house and bunches his dolls together in one big happy family, instead of having them scattered all over town, but The Brain says this idea is no good.

'In the first place,' he says, 'they do not know about each other, except Doris and Cynthia and Bobby know about Charlotte, although she does not know about them. They each think they are the only one with me. So if I corral them all together they will be jealous of each other over my love. Anyway,' The Brain says, 'such an arrangement will be very immoral and against the law. No,' he says, 'it is better to have them in different spots, because think of the many homes it gives me to go to in case I wish to go home. In fact,' The Brain says, 'I guess I have more homes to go to than any other guy on Broadway.'

Well, this may be true, but what The Brain wants with a lot of different homes is a very great mystery on Broadway, because he seldom goes home, anyway, his idea in not going home being that something may happen in this town while he is at home that he is not in on. The Brain seldom goes anywhere in particular. He never goes out in public with any one of his dolls, except maybe once or twice a year with Charlotte, his ever-loving wife, and finally he even stops going with her because Doris Clare says it does not look good to Doris's personal friends.

The Brain marries Charlotte long before he becomes the biggest guy in gambling operations in the East, and a millionaire two or three times over, but he is never much of a hand to sit around home and chew the fat with his ever-loving wife, as husbands often do. Furthermore, when he is poor he has to live in a neighbourhood which is too far away for it to be convenient for him to go home, so finally he gets out of the habit of going there.

But Charlotte is not such a doll as cares to spend more than one or two years looking at the pictures on the wall, because it seems the pictures on the wall are nothing but pictures of cows in the meadows and houses covered with snow, so she does not go home any more than necessary, either, and has her own friends and is very happy indeed, especially after The Brain gets so he can send in right along.

I will say one thing about The Brain and his dolls: he never picks a crow. He has a very good eye for faces and shapes, and even Charlotte, his ever-loving wife, is not a crow, although she is not as young as she used to be. As for Doris Clare, she is one of the great beauties on the Ziegfeld roof in her day, and while her day is by no means yesterday, or even the day before, Doris holds on pretty well in the matter of looks. Giving her a shade the best of it, I will say that Doris is thirty-two or -three, but she has plenty of zing left in her, at that, and her hair remains very blonde, no matter what.

In fact, The Brain does not care much if his dolls are blonde or brunette, because Cynthia Harris's hair is as black as the inside of a wolf, while Bobby Baker is betwixt and between, her hair being a light brown. Cynthia Harris is more of a Johnny-come-lately than Doris, being out of Mr Earl Carroll's

'Vanities', and I hear she first comes to New York as Miss Somebody in one of these beauty contests which she will win hands down if one of the judges does not get a big wink from a Miss Somebody Else.

Of course, Cynthia is doing some winking herself at this time, but it seems that she picks a guy to wink at thinking he is one of the judges, when he is nothing but a newspaperman and has no say whatever about the decision.

Well, Mr Earl Carroll feels sorry for Cynthia, so he puts her in the 'Vanities' and lets her walk around raw, and The Brain sees her, and the next thing anybody knows she is riding in a big foreign automobile the size of a rum chaser, and is chucking a terrible swell.

Personally, I always consider Bobby Baker the smartest of all The Brain's dolls, because she is just middling as to looks and she does not have any of the advantages of life like Doris Clare and Cynthia Harris, such as jobs on the stage where they can walk around showing off their shapes to guys such as The Brain. Bobby Baker starts off as nothing but a private secretary to a guy in Wall Street, and naturally she is always wearing clothes, or anyway, as many clothes as an ordinary doll wears nowadays, which is not so many, at that.

It seems that The Brain once has some business with the guy Bobby works for and happens to get talking to Bobby, and she tells him how she always wishes to meet him, what with hearing and reading about him, and how he is just as handsome and romantic-looking as she always pictures him to herself.

Now I wish to say I will never call any doll a liar, being at all times a gentleman, and for all I know, Bobby Baker may really think The Brain is handsome and romantic-looking, but personally I figure if she is not lying to him, she is at least a little excited when she makes such a statement to The Brain. The best you can give The Brain at this time is that he is very well dressed.

He is maybe forty years old, give or take a couple of years, and he is commencing to get a little bunchy about the middle, what with sitting down at card-tables so much and never taking any exercise outside of walking guys such as me up and down in front of Mindy's for a few hours every night. He has a clean-looking face, always very white around the gills, and he has nice teeth and a nice smile when he wishes to smile, which is never at guys who owe him dough.

And I will say for The Brain he has what is called personality. He tells a story well, although he is always the hero of any story he tells, and he knows how to make himself agreeable to dolls in many ways. He has a pretty fair sort of education, and while dolls such as Cynthia and Doris and maybe Charlotte, too, will rather have a charge account at Cartier's than all the education in Yale and Harvard put together, it seems that Bobby Baker likes highbrow gab, so naturally she gets plenty of same from The Brain.

Well, pretty soon Bobby is riding around in a car bigger than Cynthia's, though neither is as big as Doris's car, and all the neighbours' children over in Flatbush, which is where Bobby hails from, are very jealous of her and running around spreading gossip about her, but keeping their eyes open for big cars themselves. Personally, I always figure The Brain lowers himself socially by taking up with a doll from Flatbush, especially as Bobby Baker soon goes in for literary guys, such as newspaper scribes and similar characters around Greenwich Village.

But there is no denying Bobby Baker is a very smart little doll, and in the four or five years she is one of The Brain's dolls, she gets more dough out of him than all the others put together, because she is always telling him how much she loves him, and saying she cannot do without him, while Doris Clare and Cynthia Harris sometimes forget to mention this more than once or twice a month.

Now what happens early one morning but a guy by the name of Daffy Jack hauls off and sticks a shiv in The Brain's left side. It seems that this is done at the request of a certain party by the name of Homer Swing, who owes The Brain plenty of dough in a gambling transaction, and who becomes very indignant when The Brain presses him somewhat for payment. It seems that Daffy Jack, who is considered a very good shiv artist, aims at The Brain's heart, but misses it by a couple of inches, leaving The Brain with a very bad cut in his side which calls for some stitching.

Big Nig, the crap shooter, and I are standing at Fifty-second Street and Seventh Avenue along about 2 a.m. speaking of not much, when The Brain comes stumbling out of Fifty-second Street, and falls in Big Nig's arms, practically ruining a brand-new topcoat which Big Nig pays sixty bucks for a few days back with the blood that is coming out of the cut. Naturally, Big Nig is indignant about this, but we can see that it is no time to be speaking to The Brain about such matters. We can see that The Brain is carved up quite some, and is in a bad way.

Of course, we are not greatly surprised at seeing The Brain in this condition, because for years he is practically no price around this town, what with this guy and that being anxious to do something or other to him, but we are never expecting to see him carved up like a turkey. We are expecting to see him with a few slugs in him, and both Big Nig and me are very angry to think that there are guys around who will use such instruments as a knife on anybody.

But while we are thinking it over, The Brain says to me like this:

'Call Hymie Weissberger, and Doc Frisch,' he says, 'and take me home.'

Naturally, a guy such as The Brain wishes his lawyer before he wishes his doctor, and Hymie Weissberger is The Brain's mouthpiece, and a very sure-footed guy, at that.

'Well,' I say, 'we better take you to a hospital where you can get good attention at once.'

'No,' The Brain says. 'I wish to keep this secret. It will be a bad thing for me right now to have this get out, and if you take me to a hospital they must report it to the coppers. Take me home.'

Naturally, I say which home, being somewhat confused about The Brain's homes, and he seems to study a minute as if this is a question to be well thought out.

'Park Avenue,' The Brain says finally, so Big Nig stops a taxicab, and we help The Brain into the cab and tell the jockey to take us to the apartment house on Park Avenue near Sixty-fourth where The Brain's ever-loving wife Charlotte lives.

When we get there, I figure it is best for me to go up first and break the news gently to Charlotte, because I can see what a shock it is bound to be to any ever-loving wife to have her husband brought home in the early hours of the morning all shivved up.

Well, the door man and the elevator guy in the apartment house give me an argument about going up to The Brain's apartment, saying a blow out of some kind is going on there, but after I explain to them that The Brain is sick, they let me go. A big fat butler comes to the door of the apartment when I ring, and I can see there are many dolls and guys in evening clothes in the apartment, and somebody is singing very loud.

The butler tries to tell me I cannot see Charlotte, but I finally convince him it is best, so by and by she comes to the door, and a very pleasant sight she is, at that, with jewellery all over her. I stall around awhile, so as not to alarm her too much, and then I tell her The Brain meets with an accident and that we have him outside in a cab, and ask her where we shall put him.

'Why,' she says, 'put him in a hospital, of course. I am entertaining some very important people tonight, and I cannot have them disturbed by bringing in a hospital patient. Take him to hospital, and tell him I will come and see him to-morrow and bring him some broth.'

I try to explain to her that The Brain does not need any broth, but a nice place to lie down in, but finally she gets very testy with me and shuts the door in my face, saying as follows:

'Take him to a hospital, I tell you. This is a ridiculous hour for him to be coming home, anyway. It is twenty years since he comes home so early.'

Then as I am waiting for the elevator, she opens the door again just a little bit and says:

'By the way, is he hurt bad?'

I say we do not know how bad he is hurt, and she shuts the door again, and I go back to the cab again, thinking what a heartless doll she is, although I can see where it will be very inconvenient for her to bust up her party, at that.

The Brain is lying back in the corner of the cab, his eyes half-closed, and by this time it seems that Big Nig stops the blood somewhat with a handkerchief, but The Brain acts somewhat weak to me. He sort of rouses himself when I climb in the cab, and when I tell him his ever-loving wife is not home he smiles a bit and whispers:

'Take me to Doris.'

Now Doris lives in a big apartment house away over on West Seventy-second Street near the Drive, and I tell the taxi jockey to go there while The Brain seems to slide off into a doze. Then Big Nig leans over to me and says to me like this:

'No use taking him there,' Big Nig says. 'I see Doris going out tonight all dressed up in her ermine coat with this actor guy, Jack Walen, she is struck on. It is a very great scandal around and about the way they carry on. Let us take him to Cynthia,' Nig says. 'She is a very large-hearted doll who will be very glad to take him in.'

Now Cynthia Harris has a big suite of rooms that cost fifteen G's a year in a big hotel just off Fifth Avenue, Cynthia being a doll who likes to be downtown so if she hears of anything coming off anywhere she can get there very rapidly. When we arrive at the hotel I call her on the house 'phone and tell her I must see her about something very important, so Cynthia says for me to come up.

It is now maybe three-fifteen, and I am somewhat surprised to find Cynthia home, at that, but there she is, and looking very beautiful indeed in a négligé with her hair hanging down, and I can see that The Brain is no chump when it comes to picking them. She gives me a hello pleasant enough, but as soon as I explain what I am there for, her kisser gets very stern and she says to me like this:

'Listen,' she says, 'I got trouble enough around this joint, what with two guys getting in a fight over me at a little gathering I have here last night and the house copper coming to split them out, and I do not care to have any more. Suppose it gets out that The Brain is here? What will the newspapers print about me? Think of my reputation!'

Well, in about ten minutes I can see there is no use arguing with her, because she can talk faster than I can, and mostly she talks about what a knock it will be to her reputation if she takes The Brain in, so I leave her standing at the door in her négligé, still looking very beautiful, at that.

There is now nothing for us to do but take The Brain to Bobby Baker, who lives in a duplex apartment in Sutton Place over by the East River, where the swells set up a colony of nice apartments in the heart of an old tenement-house neighbourhood, and as we are on our way there with The Brain lying back in the cab just barely breathing, I say to Big Nig like this:

'Nig,' I say, 'when we get to Bobby's, we will carry The Brain in without asking her first and just dump him on her so she cannot refuse to take him in, although,' I say, 'Bobby Baker is a nice little doll, and I am pretty sure she will do anything she can for him, especially,' I say, 'since he pays fifty G's for this apartment we are going to.'

So when the taxicab stops in front of Bobby's house, Nig and I take The Brain out of the cab and lug him between us up to the door of Bobby's apartment, where I ring the bell. Bobby opens the door herself, and I happen to see a guy's legs zip into a room in the apartment behind her, although of course there is nothing wrong in such a sight, even though the guy's legs are in pink pyjamas.

Naturally, Bobby is greatly astonished to see us with The Brain dangling between us, but she does not invite us in as I explain to her that The Brain is stabbed and that his last words are for us to take him to his Bobby. Furthermore, she does not let me finish my story which will be very sad indeed, if she keeps on listening.

'If you do not take him away from here at once,' Bobby says, before I am down to the pathetic part, 'I will call the cops and you guys will be arrested on suspicion that you know something about how he gets hurt.'

Then she slams the door on us, and we lug The Brain back down the stairs into the street, because all of a sudden it strikes us that Bobby is right, and if The Brain is found in our possession all stabbed up, and he happens to croak, we are in a very tough spot, because the cops just naturally love to refuse to believe guys like Big Nig and me, no matter what we say.

Furthermore, the same idea must hit the taxicab jockey after we lift The Brain out of the cab, because he is nowhere to be seen, and there we are away over by the East River in the early morning, with no other taxis in sight, and a cop liable to happen along any minute.

Well, there is nothing for us to do but get away from there, so Big Nig and I start moving, with me carrying The Brain's feet, and Big Nig his head. We get several blocks away from Sutton Place, going very slow and hiding in dark doorways when we hear anybody coming, and now we are in a section of tenement houses, when all of a sudden up out of the basement of one of these tenements pops a doll.

She sees us before we can get in a dark place, and she seems to have plenty of nerve for a doll, because she comes right over to us and looks at Big Nig and me, and then looks at The Brain, who loses his hat somewhere along the line, so his pale face is plain to be seen by even the dim street light.

'Why,' the doll says, 'it is the kind gentleman who gives me the five dollars for the apple – the money that buys the medicine that saves my Joey's life. What is the matter?'

'Well,' I say to the doll, who is still raggedy and still red-headed, 'there is nothing much the matter except if we do not get him somewhere soon, this guy will up and croak on us.'

'Bring him into my house,' she says, pointing to the joint she just comes out of. 'It is not much of a place, but you can let him rest there until you get help. I am just going over here to a drug store to get some more medicine for Joey, although he is out of danger now, thanks to this gentleman.'

So we lug The Brain down the basement steps with the doll leading the way, and we follow her into a room that smells like a Chinese laundry and seems to be full of kids sleeping on the floor. There is only one bed in the room, and it is not much of a bed any way you take it, and there seems to be a kid in this bed, too, but the red-headed doll rolls this kid over to one side of the bed and motions us to lay The Brain alongside of the kid. Then she gets a wet rag and stars bathing The Brain's noggin.

He finally opens his eyes and looks at the red-headed raggedy doll, and she grins at him very pleasant. When I think things over afterwards, I figure The Brain is conscious of much of what is going on when we are packing him around, although he does not say anything, maybe because he is too weak. Anyway, he turns his head to Big Nig, and says to him like this:

'Bring Weissberger and Frisch as quick as you can,' he says. 'Anyway, get Weissberger. I do not know how bad I am hurt, and I must tell him some things.'

Well, The Brain is hurt pretty bad, as it turns out, and in fact he never gets well, but he stays in the basement dump until he dies three days later, with the red-headed raggedy doll nursing him alongside her sick kid Joey, because the croaker, old Doc Frisch, says it is no good moving The Brain, and may only make him pop off sooner. In fact, Doc Frisch is much astonished that The Brain lives at all, considering the way we lug him around.

I am present at The Brain's funeral at Wiggins's Funeral Parlours, like everybody else on Broadway, and I wish to say I never see more flowers in all my life. They are all over the casket and kneedeep on the floor, and some of the pieces must cost plenty, the price of flowers being what they are in this town nowadays. In fact, I judge it is the size and cost of the different pieces that makes me notice a little bundle of faded red carnations not much bigger than your fist that is laying alongside a pillow of violets the size of a horse blanket.

There is a small card tied to the carnations, and it says on this card, as follows: 'To a kind gentleman', and it comes to my mind that out of all the thousands of dollars' worth of flowers there, these faded carnations represent the only true sincerity. I mention this to Big Nig, and he says the chances are I am right, but that even true sincerity is not going to do The Brain any good where he is going.

Anybody will tell you that for off-hand weeping at a funeral The Brain's ever-loving wife Charlotte does herself very proud indeed, but she is not one-two-seven with Doris Clare, Cynthia Harris, and Bobby Baker. In fact, Bobby Baker weeps so loud that there is some talk of heaving her out of the funeral altogether.

However, I afterwards hear that loud as they are at the funeral, it is nothing to the weep they all put on when it comes out that The Brain has Hymie Weissberger draw up a new will while he is dying and leaves all his dough to the red-headed raggedy doll, whose name seems to be O'Halloran, and who is the widow of a bricklayer and has five kids.

Well, at first all the citizens along Broadway say it is a wonderful thing for The Brain to do, and serves his ever-loving wife and Doris and Cynthia and Bobby just right; and from the way one and all speaks you will think they are going to build a monument to The Brain for his generosity to the red-headed raggedy doll.

But about two weeks after he is dead, I hear citizens saying the chances are the red-headed raggedy doll is nothing but one of The Brain's old-time dolls, and that maybe the kids are his and that he leaves them the dough because his conscience hurts him at the finish, for this is the way Broadway is. But personally I know it cannot be true, for if there is one thing The Brain never has it is a conscience.

Dream Street Rose

Of an early evening when there is nothing much doing anywhere else, I go around to Good Time Charley's little speak in
West Forty-seventh Street that he calls the Gingham Shoppe,
and play a little klob with Charley, because business is quiet in
the Gingham Shoppe at such an hour, and Charley gets very
lonesome.

He once has a much livelier spot in Forty-eighth Street that
he calls the Crystal Room, but one night a bunch of G-guys
step into the joint and bust it wide open, besides confiscating
all of Charley's stock of merchandise. It seems that these G-
guys are members of a squad that comes on from Washington,
and being strangers in the city they do not know that Good
Time Charley's joint is not supposed to be busted up, so they
go ahead and bust it, just the same as if it is any other joint.

Well, this action causes great indignation in many quarters,
and a lot of citizens advise Charley to see somebody about
it. But Charley says no. Charley says if this is the way the
government is going to treat him after the way he walks himself
bow-legged over in France with the Rainbow Division, making
the Germans hard to catch, why, all right. But he is not going
to holler copper about it, although Charley says he has his own
opinion of Mr Hoover, at that.

Personally, I greatly admire Charley for taking the disaster
so calmly, especially as it catches him with very few potatoes.
Charley is a great hand for playing the horses with any dough
he makes out of the Crystal Room, and this particular season
the guys who play the horses are being murdered by the
bookies all over the country, and are in terrible distress.

So I know if Charley is not plumb broke that he has a

terrible crack across his belly, and I am not surprised that I do not see him for a couple of weeks after the government guys knock off the Crystal Room. I hear rumours that he is at home reading the newspapers very carefully every day, especially the obituary notices, for it seems that Charley figures that some of the G-guys may be tempted to take a belt or two at the merchandise they confiscate, and Charley says if they do, he is even for life.

Finally I hear that Charley is seen buying a bolt of gingham in Bloomington's one day, so I know he will be in action again very soon, for all Charley needs to go into action is a bolt of gingham and a few bottles of Golden Wedding. In fact, I know Charley to go into action without the gingham, but as a rule he likes to drape a place of business with gingham to make it seem more homelike to his customers, and I wish to say that when it comes to draping gingham, Charley can make a sucker of Joseph Urban, or anybody else.

Well, when I arrive at the Gingham Shoppe this night I am talking about, which is around ten o'clock, I find Charley in a very indignant state of mind, because an old tomato by the name of Dream Street Rose comes in and tracks up his floor, just after Charley gets through mopping it up, for Charley does his mopping in person, not being able as yet to afford any help.

Rose is sitting at a table in a corner, paying no attention to Charley's remarks about wiping her feet on the Welcome mat at the door before she comes in, because Rose knows there is no Welcome mat at Charley's door, anyway, but I can see where Charley has a right to a few beefs, at that, as she leaves a trail of black hoofprints across the clean floor as if she is walking around in mud somewhere before she comes in, although I do not seem to remember that it is raining when I arrive.

Now this Dream Street Rose is an old doll of maybe fifty-odd, and is a very well-known character around and about, as she is wandering through the Forties for many a year, and especially through West Forty-seventh Street between Sixth and Seventh Avenues, and this block is called Dream Street. And the reason it is called Dream Street is because in this block are many characters of one kind and another who always seem to be dreaming of different matters.

In Dream Street there are many theatrical hotels, and rooming houses, and restaurants, and speaks, including Good Time Charley's Gingham Shoppe, and in the summer time the characters I mention sit on the stoops or lean against the railings along Dream Street, and the gab you hear sometimes sounds very dreamy indeed. In fact, it sometimes sounds very pipe-dreamy.

Many actors, male and female, and especially vaudeville actors, live in the hotels and rooming houses, and vaudeville actors, both male and female, are great hands for sitting around dreaming out loud about how they will practically assassinate the public in the Palace if ever they get a chance.

Furthermore, in Dream Street are always many hand-bookies and horse players, who sit on the church steps on the cool side of Dream Street in the summer and dream about big killings on the races, and there are also nearly always many fight managers, and sometimes fighters, hanging out in front of the restaurants, picking their teeth and dreaming about winning championships of the world, although up to this time no champion of the world has yet come out of Dream Street.

In this street you see burlesque dolls, and hoofers, and guys who write songs, and saxophone players, and newsboys, and newspaper scribes, and taxi drivers, and blind guys, and midgets, and blondes with Pomeranian pooches, or maybe French poodles, and guys with whiskers, and night-club entertainers, and I do not know what all else. And all of these characters are interesting to look at, and some of them are very interesting to talk to, although if you listen to several I know long enough, you may get the idea that they are somewhat daffy, especially the horse players.

But personally I consider all horse players more or less daffy anyway. In fact, the way I look at it, if a guy is not daffy he will not be playing the horses.

Now this Dream Street Rose is a short, thick-set, square-looking old doll, with a square pan, and square shoulders, and she has heavy iron-grey hair that she wears in a square bob, and she stands very square on her feet. In fact, Rose is the squarest-looking doll I ever see, and she is as strong and lively as Jim Londos, the wrestler. In fact, Jim Londos will never be any better than 6 to 5 in my line over Dream Street Rose, if she is in any kind of shape.

Nobody in this town wishes any truck with Rose if she has a few shots of grog in her, and especially Good Time Charley's grog, for she can fight like the dickens when she is grogged up. In fact, Rose holds many a decision in this town, especially over coppers, because if there is one thing she hates and despises more than somewhat it is a copper, as coppers are always heaving her into the old can when they find her jerking citizens around and cutting up other didoes.

For many years Rose works in the different hotels along Dream Street as a chambermaid. She never works in any one hotel very long, because the minute she gets a few bobs together she likes to go out and enjoy a little recreation, such as visiting around the speaks, although she is about as welcome in most speaks as a G-guy with a search warrant. You see, nobody can ever tell when Rose may feel like taking the speak apart, and also the customers.

She never has any trouble getting a job back in any hotel she ever works in, for Rose is a wonderful hand for making up beds, although several times, when she is in a hurry to get off, I hear she makes up beds with guests still in them, which causes a few mild beefs to the management, but does not bother Rose. I speak of this matter only to show you that she is a very quaint character indeed, and full of zest.

Well, I sit down to play klob with Good Time Charley, but about this time several customers come into the Gingham Shoppe, so Charley has to go and take care of them, leaving me alone. And while I am sitting there alone I hear Dream Street Rose mumbling to herself over in the corner, but I pay no

attention to her, although I wish to say I am by no means
unfriendly with Rose.

In fact, I say hello to her at all times, and am always very
courteous to her, as I do not wish to have her bawling me out
in public, and maybe circulating rumours about me, as she is
apt to do, if she feels I am snubbing her.

Finally I notice her motioning to me to come over to her
table, and I go over at once and sit down, because I can see that
Rose is well grogged up at this time, and I do not care to have
her attracting my attention by chucking a cuspidor at me. She
offers me a drink when I sit down, but of course I never drink
anything that is sold in Good Time Charley's, as a personal
favour to Charley. He says he wishes to retain my friendship.

So I just sit there saying nothing much whatever, and Rose
keeps on mumbling to herself, and I am not able to make much
of her mumbling, until finally she looks at me and says to me
like this:

'I am now going to tell you about my friend,' Rose says.

'Well, Rose,' I say, 'personally I do not care to hear about
your friend, although,' I say, 'I have no doubt that what you
wish to tell me about this friend is very interesting. But I am
here to play a little klob with Good Time Charley, and I do not
have time to hear about your friend.'

'Charley is busy selling his poison to the suckers,' Rose says.
'I am now going to tell you about my friend. It is quite a story,'
she says. 'You will listen.'

So I listen.

It is a matter of thirty-five years ago [Dream Street Rose
says] and the spot is a town in Colorado by the name of Pueblo,
where there are smelters and one thing and another. My friend
is at this time maybe sixteen or seventeen years old, and a first-
class looker in every respect. Her papa is dead, and her mamma
runs a boarding-house for the guys who work in the smelters,
and who are very hearty eaters. My friend deals them off the
arm for the guys in her mamma's boarding-house to save her
mamma the expense of a waitress.

Now among the boarders in this boarding-house are many guys who are always doing a little pitching to my friend, and trying to make dates with her to take her places, but my friend never gives them much of a tumble, because after she gets through dealing them off the arm all day her feet generally pain her too much to go anywhere on them except to the hay.

Finally, however, along comes a tall, skinny young guy from the East by the name of Frank something, who has things to say to my friend that are much more interesting than anything that has been said to her by a guy before, including such things as love and marriage, which are always very interesting subjects to any young doll.

This Frank is maybe twenty-five years old, and he comes from the East with the idea of making his fortune in the West, and while it is true that fortunes are being made in the West at this time, there is little chance that Frank is going to make any part of a fortune, as he does not care to work very hard. In fact, he does not care to work at all, being much more partial to playing a little poker, or shooting a few craps, or maybe hustling a sucker around Mike's pool room on Santa Fe Avenue, for Frank is an excellent pool player, especially when he is playing a sucker.

Now my friend is at this time a very innocent young doll, and a good doll in every respect, and her idea of love includes a nice little home, and children running here and there and around and about, and she never has a wrong thought in her life, and believes that everybody else in the world is like herself. And the chances are if this Frank does not happen along, my friend will marry a young guy in Pueblo by the name of Higginbottom, who is very fond of her indeed, and who is a decent young guy and afterwards makes plenty of potatoes in the grocery dodge.

But my friend goes very daffy over Frank and cannot see anybody but him, and the upshot of it all is she runs away with him one day to Denver, being dumb enough to believe that he means it when he tells her that he loves her and is going to marry her. Why Frank ever bothers with such a doll as my friend in the first place is always a great mystery to one and all, and the only way anybody can explain it is that she is young and fresh, and he is a heel at heart.

'Well, Rose,' I say, 'I am now commencing to see the finish of this story about your friend, and,' I say, 'it is such a story as anybody can hear in a speak at any time in ,this town, except,' I say, 'maybe your story is longer than somewhat. So I will now thank you, and excuse myself, and play a little klob with Good Time Charley.'

'You will listen,' Dream Street Rose says, looking me slap-dab in the eye.

So I listen.

Moreover, I notice now that Good Time Charley is standing behind me, bending in an ear, as it seems that his customers take the wind after a couple of slams of Good Time Charley's merchandise, a couple of slams being about all that even a very hardy customer can stand at one session.

Of course [Rose goes on] the chances are Frank never intends marrying my friend at all, and she never knows until long afterward that the reason he leads her to the parson is that the young guy from Pueblo by the name of Higginbottom catches up with them at the old Windsor Hotel where they are stopping and privately pokes a six-pistol against Frank's ribs and promises faithfully to come back and blow a hole in Frank you can throw a watermelon through if Frank tries any phenagling around with my friend.

Well, in practically no time whatever, love's young dream is over as far as my friend is concerned. This Frank turns out to be a most repulsive character indeed, especially if you are figuring him as an ever-loving husband. In fact, he is no good. He mistreats my friend in every way any guy ever thought of mistreating a doll, and besides the old established ways of mistreating a doll, Frank thinks up quite a number of new ways, being really quite ingenious in this respect.

Yes, this Frank is one hundred per cent heel.

It is not so much that he gives her a thumping now and then, because, after all, a thumping wears off, and hurts heal up, even when they are such hurts as a broken nose and fractured ribs, and once an ankle cracked by a kick. It is what he does to her heart, and to her innocence. He is by no means a good husband, and does not know how to treat an ever-loving wife with any respect, especially as he winds up by taking my friend to San Francisco and hiring her out to a very loose character there by the name of Black Emanuel, who has a dance joint on the Barbary Coast, which, at the time I am talking about, is hotter than a stove. In this joint my friend has to dance with the customers, and get them to buy beer for her and one thing and another, and this occupation is most distasteful to my friend, as she never cares for beer.

It is there Frank leaves her for good after giving her an extra big thumping for a keepsake, and when my friend tries to leave Black Emanuel's to go looking for her ever-loving husband, she is somewhat surprised to hear Black Emanuel state that he pays Frank three C's for her to remain there and continue working. Furthermore, Black Emanuel resumes the thumpings where Frank leaves off, and by and by my friend is much bewildered and down-hearted and does not care what happens to her.

Well, there is nothing much of interest in my friend's life for the next thirty-odd years, except that she finally gets so she does not mind the beer so much, and, in fact, takes quite a fondness for it, and also for light wines and Bourbon whisky, and that she comes to realize that Frank does not love her after all, in spite of what he says. Furthermore, in later years, after she drifts around the country quite some, in and out of different joints, she realizes that the chances are she will never have a nice little home, with children running here and there, and she often thinks of what a disagreeable influence Frank has on her life.

In fact, this Frank is always on her mind more than somewhat. In fact, she thinks of him night and day, and says many a prayer that he will do well. She manages to keep track of him, which is not hard to do, at that, as Frank is in New York, and is becoming quite a guy in business, and is often in the newspapers. Maybe his success is due to my friend's prayers, but the chances are it is more because he connects up with some guy who has an invention for doing something very interesting in steel, and by grabbing an interest in this invention Frank gets a shove toward plenty of potatoes. Furthermore, he is married, and is raising up a family.

About ten or twelve years ago my friend comes to New York, and by this time she is getting a little faded around the edges. She is not so old, at that, but the air of the Western and Southern joints is bad on the complexion, and beer is no good for the figure. In fact, my friend is now quite a haybag, and she does not get any better-looking in the years she spends in New York as she is practically all out of the old sex appeal, and has to do a little heavy lifting to keep eating. But she never forgets to keep praying that Frank will continue to do well, and Frank certainly does this, as he is finally spoken of everywhere very respectfully as a millionaire and a high-class guy.

In all the years she is in New York my friend never runs into Frank, as Frank is by no means accustomed to visiting the spots where my friend hangs out, but my friend goes to a lot of bother to get acquainted with a doll who is a maid for some time in Frank's town house in East Seventy-fourth Street, and through this doll my friend keeps a pretty fair line on the way Frank lives. In fact, one day when Frank and his family are absent, my friend goes to Frank's house with her friend, just to see what it looks like, and after an hour there my friend has the joint pretty well cased.

So now my friend knows through her friend that on very hot nights such as tonight Frank's family is bound to be at their country place at Port Washington, but that Frank himself is spending the night at his town house, because he wishes to work on a lot of papers of some kind. My friend knows through her friend that all of Frank's servants are at Port Washington, too, except my friend's friend, who is in charge of the town house, and Frank's valet, a guy by the name of Sloggins.

Furthermore, my friend knows through her friend that both her friend and Sloggins have a date to go to a movie at 8.30 o'clock, to be gone a couple of hours, as it seems Frank is very big-hearted about giving his servants time off for such a purpose when he is at home alone; although one night he squawks no little when my friend is out with her friend drinking a little beer, and my friend's friend loses her door key and has to ring the bell to the servants' entrance, and rousts Frank out of a sound sleep.

Naturally, my friend's friend will be greatly astonished if she ever learns that it is with this key that my friend steps into Frank's house along about nine o'clock tonight. An electric light hangs over the servants' entrance, and my friend locates the button that controls this light just inside the door and turns it off, as my friend figures that maybe Frank and his family will not care to have any of their high-class neighbours, or anyone else, see an old doll who has no better hat than she is wearing, entering or leaving their house at such an hour.

It is an old-fashioned sort of house, four or five stories high, with the library on the third floor in the rear, looking out through french windows over a nice little garden, and my friend finds Frank in the library where she expects to find him, because she is smart enough to figure that a guy who is working on papers is not apt to be doing his work in the cellar.

But Frank is not working on anything when my friend moves in on him. He is dozing in a chair by the window, and, looking at him, after all these years, she finds something of a change, indeed. He is much heavier than he is thirty-five years back, and his hair is white, but he looks pretty well to my friend, at that, as she stands there for maybe five minutes watching him. Then he seems to realize somebody is in the room, as sleeping guys will do, for his regular breathing stops with a snort, and he opens his eyes, and looks into my friend's eyes, but without hardly stirring. And finally my friend speaks to Frank as follows:

'Well, Frank,' she says, 'do you know me?'

'Yes,' he says, after a while, 'I know you. At first I think maybe you are a ghost, as I once hear something about your being dead. But,' he says, 'I see now the report is a canard. You are too fat to be a ghost.'

Well, of course, this is a most insulting crack, indeed, but my friend passes it off as she does not wish to get in any arguments with Frank at this time. She can see that he is upset more than somewhat and he keeps looking around the room as if he hopes he can see somebody else he can cut in on the conversation. In fact, he acts as if my friend is by no means a welcome visitor.

'Well, Frank,' my friend says, very pleasant, 'there you are, and here I am. I understand you are now a wealthy and prominent citizen of this town. I am glad to know this, Frank,' she says. 'You will be surprised to hear that for years and years I pray that you will do well for yourself and become a big guy in every respect, with a nice family, and everything else. I judge my prayers are answered,' she says. 'I see by the papers that you have two sons at Yale, and a daughter in Vassar, and that your ever-loving wife is getting to be very high muckymucky in society. Well, Frank,' she says, 'I am very glad. I pray something like all this will happen to you.'

Now, at such a speech, Frank naturally figures that my friend is all right, at that, and the chances are he also figures that she still has a mighty soft spot in her heart for him, just as she has in the days when she deals them off the arm to keep him in gambling and drinking money. In fact, Frank brightens up somewhat, and he says to my friend like this:

'You pray for my success?' he says. 'Why, this is very thoughtful of you, indeed. Well,' he says, 'I am sitting on top of the world. I have everything to live for.'

'Yes,' my friend says, 'and this is exactly where I pray I will find you. On top of the world,' she says, 'and with everything to live for. It is where I am when you take my life. It is where I am when you kill me as surely as if you strangle me with your hands. I always pray you will not become a bum,' my friend says, 'because a bum has nothing to live for, anyway. I want to find you liking to live, so you will hate so much to die.'

Naturally, this does not sound so good to Frank, and he begins all of a sudden to shake and shiver and to stutter somewhat.

'Why,' he says, 'what do you mean? Are you going to kill me?'

'Well,' my friend says, 'that remains to be seen. Personally,' she says, 'I will be much obliged if you will kill yourself, but it can be arranged one way or the other. However, I will explain the disadvantages of me killing you.

'The chances are,' my friend says, 'if I kill you I will be caught and a very great scandal will result, because,' she says, 'I have on my person the certificate of my marriage to you in Denver, and something tells me you never think to get a divorce. So,' she says, 'you are a bigamist.'

'I can pay,' Frank says. 'I can pay plenty.'

'Furthermore,' my friend says, paying no attention to his remark, 'I have a sworn statement from Black Emanuel about your transaction with him, for Black Emanuel gets religion before he dies from being shivved by Johnny Mizzoo, and he tries to round himself up by confessing all the sins he can think of, which are quite a lot. It is a very interesting statement,' my friend says.

'Now then,' she says, 'if you knock yourself off you will leave an unsullied, respected name. If I kill you, all the years and effort you have devoted to building up your reputation will go for nothing. You are past sixty,' my friend says, 'and any way you figure it, you do not have so very far to go. If I kill you,' she says, 'you will go in horrible disgrace, and everybody around you will feel the disgrace, no matter how much dough you leave them. Your children will hang their heads in shame. Your ever-loving wife will not like it,' my friend says.

'I wait on you a long time, Frank,' my friend says. 'A dozen times in the past twenty years I figure I may as well call on you and close up my case with you, but,' she says, 'then I always persuade myself to wait a little longer so you would rise higher and higher and life will be a bit sweeter to you. And there you are, Frank,' she says, 'and here I am.'

Well, Frank sits there as if he is knocked plumb out, and he does not answer a word; so finally my friend outs with a large John Roscoe which she is packing in the bosom of her dress, and tosses it in his lap, and speaks as follows:

'Frank,' she says, 'do not think it will do you any good to pot me in the back when I turn around, because,' she says, 'you will be worse off than ever. I leave plenty of letters scattered around in case anything happens to me. And remember,' she says, 'if you do not do this job yourself, I will be back. Sooner or later, I will be back.'

So [Dream Street Rose says] my friend goes out of the library and down the stairs, leaving Frank sprawled out in his chair, and when she reaches the first floor she hears what may be a shot in the upper part of the house, and then again maybe only a door slamming. My friend never knows for sure what it is, because a little later as she nears the servants' entrance she hears quite a commotion outside, and a guy cussing a blue streak, and a doll teeheeing, and pretty soon my friend's friend, the maid, and Sloggins, the valet, come walking in.

Well, my friend just has time to scroonch herself back in a dark corner, and they go upstairs, the guy still cussing and the doll still giggling, and my friend cannot make out what it is all about except that they come home earlier than she figures. So my friend goes tippy-toe out of the servants' entrance, to grab a taxi not far from the house and get away from this neighbourhood, and now you will soon hear of the suicide of a guy who is a millionaire, and it will be all even with my friend.

'Well, Rose,' I say, 'it is a nice long story, and full of romance and all this and that, and,' I say, 'of course I will never be ungentlemanly enough to call a lady a liar, but,' I say, 'if it is not a lie, it will do until a lie comes along.'

'All right,' Rose says. 'Anyway, I tell you about my friend. Now,' she says, 'I am going where the liquor is better, which can be any other place in town, because,' she says, 'there is no chance of liquor anywhere being any worse.'

So she goes out, making more tracks on Good Time Charley's floor, and Charley speaks most impolitely of her after she goes, and gets out his mop to clean the floor, for one thing about Charley, he is as neat as a pin, and maybe neater.

Well, along toward one o'clock I hear a newsboy in the street outside yelling something I cannot make out, because he is yelling as if he has a mouthful of mush, as newsboys are bound to do. But I am anxious to see what goes in the first race at Belmont, on account of having a first-class tip, so I poke my noggin outside Good Time Charley's and buy a paper, and across the front page, in large letters, it states that the wealthy Mr Frank Billingsworth McQuiggan knocks himself off by putting a slug through his own noggin.

It says Mr McQuiggan is found in a chair in his library as dead as a door-nail with the pistol in his lap with which he knocks himself off, and the paper states that nobody can figure what causes Mr McQuiggan to do such a thing to himself as he is in good health and has plenty of potatoes and is at the peak of his career. Then there is a lot about his history.

When Mr McQuiggan is a young fellow returning from a visit to the Pacific Coast with about two hundred dollars in his pocket after paying his railroad fare, he meets in the train Jonas Calloway, famous inventor of the Calloway steel process. Calloway, also then young, is desperately in need of funds and he offers Mr McQuiggan a third interest in his invention for what now seems the paltry sum of one hundred dollars. Mr McQuiggan accepts the offer and thus paves the way to his own fortune.

I am telling all this to Good Time Charley while he is mopping away at the floor, and finally I come on a paragraph down near the finish which goes like this: 'The body was discovered by Mr McQuiggan's faithful valet, Thomas Sloggins, at eleven o'clock. Mr McQuiggan was then apparently dead a couple of hours. Sloggins returned home shortly before ten o'clock with another servant after changing his mind about going to a movie. Instead of going to see his employer at once, as is his usual custom, Sloggins went to his own quarters and changed his clothes.

'"The light over the servants' entrance was out when I returned home," the valet said, "and in the darkness I stumbled over some scaffolding and other material left near this entrance by workmen who are to regravel the roof of the house to-morrow, upsetting all over the entranceway a large bucket of tar, much of which got on my apparel when I fell, making a change necessary before going to see Mr McQuiggan."'

Well, Good Time Charley keeps on mopping harder than ever, though finally he stops a minute and speaks to me as follows:

'Listen,' Charley says, 'understand I do not say the guy does not deserve what he gets, and I am by no means hollering copper, but,' Charley says, 'if he knocks himself off, how does it come the rod is still in his lap where Dream Street Rose says her friend tosses it? Well, never mind,' Charley says, 'but can you think of something that will remove tar from a wood floor? It positively will not mop off.'

The Old Doll's House

Now it seems that one cold winter night, a party of residents of Brooklyn comes across the Manhattan Bridge in an automobile wishing to pay a call on a guy by the name of Lance McGowan, who is well known to one and all along Broadway as a coming guy in the business world.

In fact, it is generally conceded that, barring accident, Lance will someday be one of the biggest guys in this country as an importer, and especially as an importer of such merchandise as fine liquors, because he is very bright, and has many good connections throughout the United States and Canada.

Furthermore, Lance McGowan is a nice-looking young guy and he has plenty of ticker, although some citizens say he does not show very sound business judgement in trying to move in on Angie the Ox over in Brooklyn, as Angie the Ox is an importer himself, besides enjoying a splendid trade in other lines, including artichokes and extortion.

Of course Lance McGowan is not interested in artichokes at all, and very little in extortion, but he does not see any reason why he shall not place his imports in a thriving territory such as Brooklyn, especially as his line of merchandise is much superior to anything handled by Angie the Ox.

Anyway, Angie is one of the residents of Brooklyn in the party that wishes to call on Lance McGowan, and besides Angie the party includes a guy by the name of Mockie Max, who is a very prominent character in Brooklyn, and another guy by the name of The Louse Kid, who is not so prominent, but who is considered a very promising young guy in many respects, although personally I think The Louse Kid has a very weak face.

He is supposed to be a wonderful hand with a burlap bag when anybody wishes to put somebody in such a bag, which is considered a great practical joke in Brooklyn, and in fact The Louse Kid has a burlap bag with him on the night in question, and they are figuring on putting Lance McGowan in the bag when they call on him, just for the laugh. Personally, I consider this a very crude form of humour, but then Angie the Ox and the other members of his party are very crude characters, anyway.

Well, it seems they have Lance McGowan pretty well cased, and they know that of an evening along toward ten o'clock he nearly always strolls through West Fifty-fourth street on his way to a certain spot on Park Avenue that is called the Humming Bird Club, which has a very high-toned clientele, and the reason Lance goes there is because he has a piece of the joint, and furthermore he loves to show off his shape in a tuxedo to the swell dolls.

So these residents of Brooklyn drive in their automobile along this route, and as they roll past Lance McGowan, Angie the Ox and Mockie Max let fly at Lance with a couple of sawed-offs, while The Louse Kid holds the burlap bag, figuring for all I know that Lance will be startled by the sawed-offs and will hop into the bag like a rabbit.

But Lance is by no means a sucker, and when the first blast of slugs from the sawed-offs breezes past him without hitting him, what does he do but hop over a brick wall alongside him and drop into a yard on the other side. So Angie the Ox, and Mockie Max and The Louse Kid get out of their automobile and run up close to the wall themselves because they commence figuring that if Lance McGowan starts popping at them from behind this wall, they will be taking plenty the worst of it, for of course they cannot figure Lance to be strolling about without being rodded up somewhat.

But Lance is by no means rodded up, because a rod is apt to create a bump in his shape when he has his tuxedo on, so the story really begins with Lance McGowan behind the brick wall, practically defenceless, and the reason I know this story is because Lance McGowan tells most of it to me, as Lance knows that I know his real name is Lancelot, and he feels under great obligation to me because I never mention the matter publicly.

Now, the brick wall Lance hops over is a wall around a pretty fair-sized yard, and the yard belongs to an old two-story stone house, and this house is well known to one and all in this man's town as a house of great mystery, and it is pointed out as such by the drivers of sightseeing buses.

This house belongs to an old doll by the name of Miss Abigail Ardsley, and anybody who ever reads the newspapers will tell you that Miss Abigail Ardsley has so many potatoes that it is really painful to think of, especially to people who have no potatoes whatever. In fact, Miss Abigail Ardsley has practically all the potatoes in the world, except maybe a few left over for general circulation.

These potatoes are left to her by her papa, old Waldo Ardsley, who accumulates same in the early days of this town by buying corner real estate very cheap before people realize this real estate will be quite valuable later on for fruit-juice stands and cigar stores.

It seems that Waldo is a most eccentric old bloke, and is very strict with his daughter, and will never let her marry, or even as much as look as if she wishes to marry, until finally she is so old she does not care a cuss about marrying, or anything else, and becomes very eccentric herself.

In fact, Miss Abigail Ardsley becomes so eccentric that she cuts herself off from everybody, and especially from a lot of relatives who are wishing to live off her, and any time anybody cuts themselves off from such characters they are considered very eccentric, indeed, especially by the relatives. She lives in the big house all alone, except for a couple of old servants, and it is very seldom that anybody sees her around and about, and many strange stories are told of her.

Well, no sooner is he in the yard than Lance McGowan

begins looking for a way to get out, and one way he does not wish to get out is over the wall again, because he figures Angie the Ox and his sawed-offs are bound to be waiting for him in Fifty-fourth Street. So Lance looks around to see if there is some way out of the yard in another direction, but it seems there is no such way, and pretty soon he sees the snozzle of a sawed-off come poking over the wall, with the ugly kisser of Angie the Ox behind it, looking for him, and there is Lance McGowan all cornered up in the yard, and not feeling so good, at that.

Then Lance happens to try a door on one side of the house, and the door opens at once and Lance McGowan hastens in to find himself in the living-room of the house. It is a very large living-room with very nice furniture standing around and about, and oil-paintings on the walls, and a big old grand-father's clock as high as the ceiling, and statuary here and there. In fact, it is such a nice, comfortable-looking room that Lance McGowan is greatly surprised, as he is expecting to find a regular mystery-house room such as you see in the movies, with cobwebs here and there, and everything all rotted up, and maybe Boris Karloff wandering about making strange noises.

But the only person in this room seems to be a little old doll all dressed in soft white, who is sitting in a low rocking-chair by an open fireplace in which a bright fire is going, doing some tatting.

Well, naturally Lance McGowan is somewhat startled by this scene, and he is figuring that the best thing he can do is to guzzle the old doll before she can commence yelling for the gendarmes, when she looks up at him and gives him a soft smile, and speaks to him in a soft voice, as follows:

'Good evening,' the old doll says.

Well, Lance cannot think of any reply to make to this at once, as it is certainly not a good evening for him, and he stands there looking at the old doll, somewhat dazed, when she smiles again and tells him to sit down.

So the next thing Lance knows, he is sitting there in a chair in front of the fireplace chewing the fat with the old doll as pleasant as you please, and of course the old doll is nobody but Miss Abigail Ardsley. Furthermore, she does not seem at all alarmed, or even much surprised, at seeing Lance in her house, but then Lance is never such a looking guy as is apt to scare old dolls, or young dolls either, especially when he is all slicked up.

Of course Lance knows who Miss Abigail Ardsley is, because he often reads stories in the newspapers about her the same as everybody else, and he always figures such a character must be slightly daffy to cut herself off from everybody when she has all the potatoes in the world, and there is so much fun going on, but he is very courteous to her, because after all he is a guest in her home.

'You are young,' the old doll says to Lance McGowan, looking him in the kisser. 'It is many years since a young man comes through yonder door. Ah, yes,' she says, 'so many years.'

And with this she lets out a big sigh, and looks so very sad that Lance McGowan's heart is touched.

'Forty-five years now,' the old doll says in a low voice, as if she is talking to herself. 'So young, so handsome, and so good.'

And although Lance is in no mood to listen to reminiscences at this time, the next thing he knows he is hearing a very pathetic love story, because it seems that Miss Abigail Ardsley is once all hotted up over a young guy who is nothing but a clerk in her papa's office.

It seems from what Lance McGowan gathers that there is nothing wrong with the young guy that a million bobs will not cure, but Miss Abigail Ardsley's papa is a mean old waffle, and he will never listen to her having any truck with a poor guy, so they dast not let him know how much they love each other.

But it seems that Miss Abigail Ardsley's ever-loving young guy has plenty of moxie, and every night he comes to see her after her papa goes to the hay, and she lets him in through the same side-door Lance McGowan comes through, and they sit by the fire and hold hands, and talk in low tones, and plan what they will do when the young guy makes a scratch.

Then one night it seems Miss Abigail Ardsley's papa has the stomach ache, or some such, and cannot sleep a wink, so he comes wandering downstairs looking for the Jamaica ginger, and catches Miss Abigail Ardsley and her ever-loving guy in a clutch that will win the title for any wrestler that can ever learn it.

Well, this scene is so repulsive to Miss Abigail Ardsley's papa that he is practically speechless for a minute, and then he orders the young guy out of his life in every respect, and tells him never to darken his door again, especially the side-door.

But it seems that by this time a great storm is raging outside, and Miss Abigail Ardsley begs and pleads with her papa to let the young guy at least remain until the storm subsides, but between being all sored up at the clutching scene he witnesses, and his stomach ache, Mr Ardsley is very hard-hearted, indeed, and he makes the young guy take the wind.

The next morning the poor young guy is found at the side-door frozen as stiff as a board, because it seems that the storm that is raging is the blizzard of 1888, which is a very famous event in the history of New York, although up to this time Lance McGowan never hears of it before, and does not believe it until he looks the matter up afterwards. It seems from what Miss Abigail Ardsley says that as near as anyone can make out, the young guy must return to the door seeking shelter after wandering about in the storm a while, but of course by this time her papa has the door all bolted up, and nobody hears the young guy.

'And,' Miss Abigail Ardsley says to Lance McGowan, after giving him all these details, 'I never speak to my papa again as long as he lives, and no other man ever comes in or out of yonder door, or any other door of this house, until your appearance tonight, although,' she says, 'this side-door is never locked in case such a young man comes seeking shelter.'

Then she looks at Lance McGowan in such a way that he

wonders if Miss Abigail Ardsley hears the sawed-offs going when Angie the Ox and Mockie Max are tossing slugs at him, but he is too polite to ask.

Well, all these old-time memories seem to make Miss Abigail Ardsley feel very tough, and by and by she starts to weep, and if there is one thing Lance McGowan cannot stand it is a doll weeping, even if she is nothing but an old doll. So he starts in to cheer Miss Abigail Ardsley up, and he pats her on the arm, and says to her like this:

'Why,' Lance says, 'I am greatly surprised to hear your statement about the doors around here being so little used. Why, Sweetheart,' Lance says, 'if I know there is a doll as good-looking as you in the neighbourhood, and a door un-locked, I will be busting in myself every night. Come, come, come,' Lance says, 'let us talk things over and maybe have a few laughs, because I may have to stick around here a while. Listen, Sweetheart,' he says, 'do you happen to have a drink in the joint?'

Well, at this Miss Abigail Ardsley dries her eyes, and smiles again, and then she pulls a sort of rope near her, and in comes a guy who seems about ninety years old, and who seems greatly surprised to see Lance there. In fact, he is so surprised that he is practically tottering when he leaves the room after hearing Miss Abigail Ardsley tell him to bring some wine and sand-wiches.

And the wine he brings is such wine that Lance McGowan has half a mind to send some of the lads around afterwards to see if there is any more of it in the joint, especially when he thinks of the unlocked side-door, because he can sell this kind of wine by the carat.

Well, Lance sits there with Miss Abigail Ardsley sipping wine and eating sandwiches, and all the time he is telling her stories of one kind and another, some of which he cleans up a little when he figures they may be a little too snappy for her, and by and by he has her laughing quite heartily indeed.

Finally he figures there is no chance of Angie and his sawed-offs being outside waiting for him, so he says he guesses he will be going, and Miss Abigail Ardsley personally sees him to the door, and this time it is the front door, and as Lance is leaving he thinks of something he once sees a guy do on the stage, and he takes Miss Abigail Ardsley's hand and raises it to his lips and gives it a large kiss, all of which is very surprising to Miss Abigail Ardsley, but more so to Lance McGowan when he gets to thinking about it afterwards.

Just as he figures, there is no one in sight when he gets out in the street, so he goes on over to the Humming Bird Club, where he learns that many citizens are greatly disturbed by his absence, and are wondering if he is in The Louse Kid's burlap bag, for by this time it is pretty well known that Angie the Ox and his fellow citizens of Brooklyn are around and about.

In fact, somebody tells Lance that Angie is at the moment over in Good Time Charley's little speak in West Forty-ninth Street, buying drinks for one and all, and telling how he makes Lance McGowan hop a brick wall, which of course sounds most disparaging of Lance.

Well, while Angie is still buying these drinks, and still speaking of making Lance a brick-wall hopper, all of a sudden the door of Good Time Charley's speak opens and in comes a guy with a Betsy in his hand and this guy throws four slugs into Angie the Ox before anybody can say hello.

Furthermore, the guy throws one slug into Mockie Max, and one slug into The Louse Kid, who are still with Angie the Ox, so the next thing anybody knows there is Angie as dead as a door-nail, and there is Mockie Max even deader than Angie, and there is The Louse making a terrible fuss over a slug in his leg, and nobody can remember what the guy who plugs them looks like, except a couple of stool pigeons who state that the guy looks very much like Lance McGowan.

So what happens but early the next morning Johnny Brannigan, the plain-clothes copper, puts the arm on Lance McGowan for plugging Angie the Ox, and Mockie Max and The Louse Kid, and there is great rejoicing in copper circles generally because at this time the newspapers are weighing in the sacks on the coppers quite some, claiming there is too much lawlessness going on around and about and asking why somebody is not arrested for something.

So the collar of Lance McGowan is water on the wheel of one and all because Lance is so prominent, and anybody will tell you that it looks as if it is a sure thing that Lance will be very severely punished, and maybe sent to the electric chair, although he hires Judge Goldstein, who is one of the surest-footed lawyers in this town, to defend him. But even Judge Goldstein admits that Lance is in a tough spot, especially as the newspapers are demanding justice, and printing long stories about Lance, and pictures of him, and calling him some very uncouth names.

Finally Lance himself commences to worry about his predicament, although up to this time a little thing like being charged with murder in the first degree never bothers Lance very much. And in fact he will not be bothering very much about this particular charge if he does not find the D.A. very fussy about letting him out on bail. In fact, it is nearly two weeks before he lets Lance out on bail, and all this time Lance is in the sneezer, which is a most mortifying situation to a guy as sensitive as Lance.

Well, by the time Lance's trial comes up, you can get 3 to 1 anywhere that he will be convicted, and the price goes up to 5 when the prosecution gets through with its case, and proves by the stool pigeons that at exactly twelve o'clock on the night of January 5th, Lance McGowan steps into Good Time Charley's little speak and plugs Angie the Ox, Mockie Max and The Louse Kid.

Furthermore, several other witnesses who claim they know Lance McGowan by sight testify that they see Lance in the neighbourhood of Good Time Charley's around twelve o'clock, so by the time it comes Judge Goldstein's turn to put on the defence, many citizens are saying that if he can do no more than beat the chair for Lance he will be doing a wonderful job.

Well, it is late in the afternoon when Judge Goldstein gets up and looks all around the courtroom, and without making any opening statement to the jury for the defence, as these mouthpieces usually do, he says like this:

'Call Miss Abigail Ardsley,' he says.

At first nobody quite realizes just who Judge Goldstein is calling for, although the name sounds familiar to one and all present who read the newspapers, when in comes a little old doll in a black silk dress that almost reaches the floor, and a black bonnet that makes a sort of a frame for her white hair and face.

Afterwards I read in one of the newspapers that she looks like she steps down out of an old-fashioned ivory miniature and that she is practically beautiful, but of course Miss Abigail Ardsley has so many potatoes that no newspaper dast to say she looks like an old chromo.

Anyway, she comes into the courtroom surrounded by so many old guys you will think it must be recess at the Old Men's Home, except they are all dressed up in claw-hammer coat tails, and high collars, and afterwards it turns out that they are the biggest lawyers in this town, and they all represent Miss Abigail Ardsley one way or another, and they are present to see that her interests are protected, especially from each other.

Nobody ever sees so much bowing and scraping before in a courtroom. In fact, even the judge bows, and although I am only a spectator I find myself bowing too, because the way I look at it, anybody with as many potatoes as Miss Abigail Ardsley is entitled to a general bowing. When she takes the witness-stand, her lawyers grab chairs and move up as close to her as possible, and in the street outside there is practically a riot as word goes around that Miss Abigail Ardsley is in the court, and citizens come running from every which way, hoping to get a peek at the richest old doll in the world.

Well, when all hands finally get settled down a little, Judge Goldstein speaks to Miss Abigail Ardsley as follows:

'Miss Ardsley,' he says, 'I am going to ask you just two or three questions. Kindly look at this defendant,' Judge Goldstein says, pointing at Lance McGowan, and giving Lance the office to stand up. 'Do you recognize him?'

Well, the little old doll takes a gander at Lance, and nods her head yes, and Lance gives her a large smile, and Judge Goldstein says:

'Is he a caller in your home on the night of January fifth?' Judge Goldstein asks.

'He is,' Miss Abigail Ardsley says.

'Is there a clock in the living-room in which you receive this defendant?' Judge Goldstein says.

'There is,' Miss Abigail Ardsley says. 'A large clock,' she says. 'A grandfather's clock.'

'Do you happen to notice,' Judge Goldstein says, 'and do you now recall the hour indicated by this clock when the defendant leaves your home?'

'Yes,' Miss Abigail Ardsley says, 'I do happen to notice. It is just twelve o'clock by my clock,' she says. 'Exactly twelve o'clock,' she says.

Well, this statement creates a large sensation in the courtroom, because if it is twelve o'clock when Lance McGowan leaves Miss Abigail Ardsley's house in West Fifty-fourth Street, anybody can see that there is no way he can be in Good Time Charley's little speak over five blocks away at the same minute unless he is a magician, and the judge begins peeking over his specs at the coppers in the courtroom very severe, and the cops begin scowling at the stool pigeons, and I am willing to lay plenty of 6 to 5 that the stools will wish they are never born before they hear the last of this matter from the gendarmes.

Furthermore, the guys from the D.A.'s office who are handling the prosecution are looking much embarrassed, and the jurors are muttering to each other, and right away Judge Goldstein says he moves that the case against his client be dismissed, and the judge says he is in favour of the motion, and he also says he thinks it is high time the gendarmes in this town learn to be a little careful who they are arresting for murder, and the guys from the D.A.'s office do not seem to be able to think of anything whatever to say.

So there is Lance as free as anybody, and as he starts to leave the courtroom he stops by Miss Abigail Ardsley, who is still sitting in the witness-chair surrounded by her mouthpieces, and he shakes her hand and thanks her, and while I do not hear it myself, somebody tells me afterwards that Miss Abigail Ardsley says to Lance in a low voice, like this:

'I will be expecting you again some night, young man,' she says.

'Some night, Sweetheart,' Lance says, 'at twelve o'clock.'

And then he goes on about his business, and Miss Abigail Ardsley goes on about hers; and everybody says it is certainly a wonderful thing that a doll as rich as Miss Abigail Ardsley comes forward in the interests of justice to save a guy like Lance McGowan from a wrong rap.

But of course it is just as well for Lance that Miss Abigail Ardsley does not explain to the court that when she recovers from the shock of the finding of her ever-loving young guy frozen to death, she stops all the clocks in her house at the hour she sees him last, so for forty-five years it is always twelve o'clock in her house.

Romance in the Roaring Forties

Only a rank sucker will think of taking two peeks at Dave the Dude's doll, because while Dave may stand for the first peek, figuring it is a mistake, it is a sure thing he will get sored up at the second peek, and Dave the Dude is certainly not a man to have sored up at you.

But this Waldo Winchester is one hundred per cent sucker, which is why he takes quite a number of peeks at Dave's doll. And what is more, she takes quite a number of peeks right back at him. And there you are. When a guy and a doll get to taking peeks back and forth at each other, why, there you are indeed.

This Waldo Winchester is a nice-looking young guy who writes pieces about Broadway for the *Morning Item*. He writes about the goings-on in night clubs, such as fights, and one thing and another, and also about who is running around with who, including guys and dolls.

Sometimes this is very embarrassing to people who may be married and are running around with people who are not married, but of course Waldo Winchester cannot be expected to ask one and all for their marriage certificates before he writes his pieces for the paper.

The chances are if Waldo Winchester knows Miss Billy Perry is Dave the Dude's doll, he will never take more than his first peek at her, but nobody tips him off until his second or third peek, and by this time Miss Billy Perry is taking her peeks back at him and Waldo Winchester is hooked.

In fact, he is plumb gone, and being a sucker, like I tell you, he does not care whose doll she is. Personally, I do not blame him much, for Miss Billy Perry is worth a few peeks, especially when she is out on the floor of Miss Missouri Martin's Sixteen

Hundred Club doing her tap dance. Still, I do not think the best tap-dancer that ever lives can make me take two peeks at her if I know she is Dave the Dude's doll, for Dave somehow thinks more than somewhat of his dolls.

He especially thinks plenty of Miss Billy Perry, and sends her fur coats, and diamond rings, and one thing and another, which she sends back to him at once, because it seems she does not take presents from guys. This is considered most surprising all along Broadway, but people figure the chances are she has some other angle.

Anyway, this does not keep Dave the Dude from liking her just the same, and so she is considered his doll by one and all, and is respected accordingly until this Waldo Winchester comes along.

It happens that he comes along while Dave the Dude is off in the Modoc on a little run down to the Bahamas to get some goods for his business, such as Scotch and champagne, and by the time Dave gets back Miss Billy Perry and Waldo Winchester are at the stage where they sit in corners between her numbers and hold hands.

Of course nobody tells Dave the Dude about this, because they do not wish to get him excited. Not even Miss Missouri Martin tells him, which is most unusual because Miss Missouri Martin, who is sometimes called 'Mizzoo' for short, tells everything she knows as soon as she knows it, which is very often before it happens.

You see the idea is when Dave the Dude is excited he may blow somebody's brains out, and the chances are it will be nobody's brains but Waldo Winchester's, although some claim that Waldo Winchester has no brains or he will not be hanging around Dave the Dude's doll.

I know Dave is very, very fond of Miss Billy Perry, because I hear him talk to her several times, and he is most polite to her and never gets out of line in her company by using cuss words, or anything like this. Furthermore, one night when One-eyed Solly Abrahams is a little stewed up he refers to Miss Billy

Perry as a broad, meaning no harm whatever, for this is the way many of the boys speak of the dolls.

But right away Dave the Dude reaches across the table and bops One-eyed Solly right in the mouth, so everybody knows from then on that Dave thinks well of Miss Billy Perry. Of course Dave is always thinking fairly well of some doll as far as this goes, but it is seldom he gets to bopping guys in the mouth over them.

Well, one night what happens but Dave the Dude walks into the Sixteen Hundred Club, and there in the entrance, what does he see but this Waldo Winchester and Miss Billy Perry kissing each other back and forth friendly. Right away Dave reaches for the old equalizer to shoot Waldo Winchester, but it seems Dave does not happen to have the old equalizer with him, not expecting to have to shoot anybody this particular evening.

So Dave the Dude walks over and, as Waldo Winchester hears him coming and lets go his strangle-hold on Miss Billy Perry, Dave nails him with a big right hand on the chin. I will say for Dave the Dude that he is a fair puncher with his right hand, though his left is not so good, and he knocks Waldo Winchester bow-legged. In fact, Waldo folds right up on the floor.

Well, Miss Billy Perry lets out a screech you can hear clear to the Battery and runs over to where Waldo Winchester lights, and falls on top of him squalling very loud. All anybody can make out of what she says is that Dave the Dude is a big bum, although Dave is not so big, at that, and that she loves Waldo Winchester.

Dave walks over and starts to give Waldo Winchester the leather, which is considered customary in such cases, but he seems to change his mind, and instead of booting Waldo around, Dave turns and walks out of the joint looking very black and mad, and the next anybody hears of him he is over in the Chicken Club doing plenty of drinking.

This is regarded as a very bad sign indeed, because while

everybody goes to the Chicken Club now and then to give Tony Bertazzola, the owner, a friendly play, very few people care to do any drinking there, because Tony's liquor is not meant for anybody to drink except the customers.

Well, Miss Billy Perry gets Waldo Winchester on his pegs again, and wipes his chin off with her handkerchief, and by and by he is all okay except for a big lump on his chin. And all the time she is telling Waldo Winchester what a big bum Dave the Dude is, although afterwards Miss Missouri Martin gets hold of Miss Billy Perry and puts the blast on her plenty for chasing a two-handed spender such as Dave the Dude out of the joint.

'You are nothing but a little sap,' Miss Missouri Martin tells Miss Billy Perry. 'You cannot get the right time off this newspaper guy, while everybody knows Dave the Dude is a very fast man with a dollar.'

'But I love Mr Winchester,' says Miss Billy Perry. 'He is so romantic. He is not a bootlegger and a gunman like Dave the Dude. He puts lovely pieces in the paper about me, and he is a gentleman at all times.'

Now of course Miss Missouri Martin is not in a position to argue about gentlemen, because she meets very few in the Sixteen Hundred Club and anyway, she does not wish to make Waldo Winchester mad as he is apt to turn around and put pieces in his paper that will be a knock to the joint, so she lets the matter drop.

Miss Billy Perry and Waldo Winchester go on holding hands between her numbers, and maybe kissing each other now and then, as young people are liable to do, and Dave the Dude plays the chill for the Sixteen Hundred Club and everything seems to be all right. Naturally we are all very glad there is no more trouble over the proposition, because the best Dave can get is the worst of it in a jam with a newspaper guy.

Personally, I figure Dave will soon find himself another doll and forget all about Miss Billy Perry, because now that I take another peek at her, I can see where she is just about the same as any other tap-dancer, except that she is red-headed. Tap-dancers are generally blackheads, but I do not know why.

Moosh, the doorman at the Sixteen Hundred Club, tells me Miss Missouri Martin keeps plugging for Dave the Dude with Miss Billy Perry in a quiet way, because he says he hears Miss Missouri Martin make the following crack one night to her: 'Well, I do not see any Simple Simon on your lean and linger.'

This is Miss Missouri Martin's way of saying she sees no diamond on Miss Billy Perry's finger, for Miss Missouri Martin is an old experienced doll, who figures if a guy loves a doll he will prove it with diamonds. Miss Missouri Martin has many diamonds herself, though how any guy can ever get himself heated up enough about Miss Missouri Martin to give her diamonds is more than I can see.

I am not a guy who goes around much, so I do not see Dave the Dude for a couple of weeks, but late one Sunday afternoon little Johnny McGowan, who is one of Dave's men, comes and says to me like this: 'What do you think? Dave grabs the scribe a little while ago and is taking him out for an airing!'

Well, Johnny is so excited it is some time before I can get him cooled out enough to explain. It seems that Dave the Dude gets his biggest car out of the garage and sends his driver, Wop Joe, over to the *Item* office where Waldo Winchester works, with a message that Miss Billy Perry wishes to see Waldo right away at Miss Missouri Martin's apartment on Fifty-ninth Street.

Of course this message is nothing but the phonus bolonus, but Waldo drops in for it and gets in the car. Then Wop Joe drives him up to Miss Missouri Martin's apartment, and who gets in the car there but Dave the Dude. And away they go.

Now this is very bad news indeed, because when Dave the Dude takes a guy out for an airing the guy very often does not come back. What happens to him I never ask, because the best a guy can get by asking questions in this man's town is a bust in the nose.

But I am much worried over this proposition, because I like

Dave the Dude, and I know that taking a newspaper guy like Waldo Winchester out for an airing is apt to cause talk, especially if he does not come back. The other guys that Dave the Dude takes out for airings do not mean much in particular, but here is a guy who may produce trouble, even if he is a sucker, on account of being connected with a newspaper.

I know enough about newspapers to know that by and by the editor or somebody will be around wishing to know where Waldo Winchester's pieces about Broadway are, and if there are no pieces from Waldo Winchester, the editor will wish to know why. Finally it will get around to where other people will wish to know, and after a while many people will be running around saying: 'Where is Waldo Winchester?'

And if enough people in this town get to running around saying where is So-and-so, it becomes a great mystery and the newspapers hop on the cops and the cops hop on everybody, and by and by there is so much heat in town that it is no place for a guy to be.

But what is to be done about this situation I do not know. Personally, it strikes me as very bad indeed, and while Johnny goes away to do a little telephoning, I am trying to think up some place to go where people will see me, and remember afterwards that I am there in case it is necessary for them to remember.

Finally Johnny comes back, very excited, and says: 'Hey, the Dude is up at the Woodcock Inn on the Pelham Parkway, and he is sending out the word for one and all to come at once. Good Time Charley Bernstein just gets the wire and tells me. Something is doing. The rest of the mob are on their way, so let us be moving.'

But here is an invitation which does not strike me as a good thing at all. The way I look at it, Dave the Dude is no company for a guy like me at this time. The chances are he either does something to Waldo Winchester already, or is getting ready to do something to him which I wish no part of.

Personally, I have nothing against newspaper guys, not even

the ones who write pieces about Broadway. If Dave the Dude wishes to do something to Waldo Winchester, all right, but what is the sense of bringing outsiders into it? But the next thing I know, I am in Johnny McGowan's roadster, and he is zipping along very fast indeed, paying practically no attention to traffic lights or anything else.

As we go busting out the Concourse, I get to thinking the situation over, and I figure that Dave the Dude probably keeps thinking about Miss Billy Perry, and drinking liquor such as they sell in the Chicken Club, until finally he blows his topper. The way I look at it, only a guy who is off his nut will think of taking a newspaper guy out for an airing over a doll, when dolls are a dime a dozen in this man's town.

Still, I remember reading in the papers about a lot of different guys who are considered very sensible until they get tangled up with a doll, and maybe loving her, and the first thing anybody knows they hop out of windows, or shoot themselves, or somebody else, and I can see where even a guy like Dave the Dude may go daffy over a doll.

I can see that little Johnny McGowan is worried, too, but he does not say much, and we pull up in front of the Woodcock Inn in no time whatever, to find a lot of other cars there ahead of us, some of which I recognize as belonging to different parties.

The Woodcock Inn is what is called a road house, and is run by Big Nig Skolsky, a very nice man indeed, and a friend of everybody's. It stands back a piece off the Pelham Parkway and is a very pleasant place to go to, what with Nig having a good band and a floor show with a lot of fair-looking dolls, and everything else a man can wish for a good time. It gets a nice play from nice people, although Nig's liquor is nothing extra.

Personally, I never go there much, because I do not care for road houses, but it is a great spot for Dave the Dude when he is pitching parties, or even when he is only drinking single-handed. There is a lot of racket in the joint as we drive up, and who comes out to meet us but Dave the Dude himself with a big hello. His face is very red, and he seems heated up no little, but he does not look like a guy who is meaning any harm to anybody, especially a newspaper guy.

'Come in, guys!' Dave the Dude yells. 'Come right in!'

So we go in, and the place is full of people sitting at tables, or out on the floor dancing, and I see Miss Missouri Martin with all her diamonds hanging from her in different places, and Good Time Charley Bernstein, and Feet Samuels, and Tony Bertazzola, and Skeets Boliver, and Nick the Greek, and Rochester Red, and a lot of other guys and dolls from around and about.

In fact, it looks as if everybody from all the joints on Broadway are present, including Miss Billy Perry, who is all dressed up in white and is lugging a big bundle of orchids and so forth, and who is giggling and smiling and shaking hands and going on generally. And finally I see Waldo Winchester, the scribe, sitting at a ringside table all by himself, but there is nothing wrong with him as far as I can see. I mean, he seems to be all in one piece so far.

'Dave,' I say to Dave the Dude, very quiet, 'what is coming off here? You know a guy cannot be too careful what he does around this town, and I will hate to see you tangled up in anything right now.'

'Why,' Dave says, 'what are you talking about? Nothing is coming off here but a wedding, and it is going to be the best wedding anybody on Broadway ever sees. We are waiting for the preacher now.'

'You mean somebody is going to be married?' I ask, being now somewhat confused.

'Certainly,' Dave the Dude says. 'What do you think? What is the idea of a wedding, anyway?'

'Who is going to be married?' I ask.

'Nobody but Billy and the scribe,' Dave says. 'This is the greatest thing I ever do in my life. I run into Billy the other night and she is crying her eyes out because she loves this scribe and wishes to marry him, but it seems the scribe has nothing he can use for money. So I tell Billy to leave it to me, because you know I love her myself so much I wish to see her happy at all times, even if she has to marry to be that way.

'So I frame this wedding party, and after they are married I am going to stake them to a few G's so they can get a good running start,' Dave says. 'But I do not tell the scribe and I do not let Billy tell him as I wish it to be a big surprise to him. I kidnap him this afternoon and bring him out here and he is scared half to death thinking I am going to scrag him.

'In fact,' Dave says, 'I never see a guy so scared. He is still so scared nothing seems to cheer him up. Go over and tell him to shake himself together, because nothing but happiness for him is coming off here.'

Well, I wish to say I am greatly relieved to think that Dave intends doing nothing worse to Waldo Winchester than getting him married up, so I go over to where Waldo is sitting. He certainly looks somewhat alarmed. He is all in a huddle with himself, and he has what you call a vacant stare in his eyes. I can see that he is indeed frightened, so I give him a jolly slap on the back and I say: 'Congratulations, pal Cheer up, the worst is yet to come!'

'You bet it is,' Waldo Winchester says, his voice so solemn I am greatly surprised.

'You are a fine-looking bridegroom,' I say. 'You look as if you are at a funeral instead of a wedding. Why do you not laugh ha-ha, and maybe take a dram or two and go to cutting up some?'

'Mister,' says Waldo Winchester, 'my wife is not going to care for me getting married to Miss Billy Perry.'

'Your wife?'I say, much astonished. 'What is this you are speaking of? How can you have any wife except Miss Billy Perry? This is great foolishness.'

'I know,' Waldo says, very sad. 'I know. But I got a wife just the same, and she is going to be very nervous when she hears about this. My wife is very strict with me. My wife does not allow me to go around marrying people. My wife is Lola

Sapola, of the Rolling Sapolas, the acrobats, and I am married
to her for five years. She is the strong lady who juggles the
other four people in the act. My wife just gets back from a
year's tour of the Interstate time, and she is at the Marx Hotel
right this minute. I am upset by this proposition.'

'Does Miss Billy Perry know about this wife?' I ask.

'No,' he says. 'No. She thinks I am single-o.'

'But why do you not tell Dave the Dude you are already
married when he brings you out here to marry you off to Miss
Billy Perry?' I ask. 'It seems to me a newspaper guy must know
it is against the law for a guy to marry several different dolls
unless he is a Turk, or some such.'

'Well,' Waldo says, 'if I tell Dave the Dude I am married
after taking his doll away from him, I am quite sure Dave will
be very much excited, and maybe do something harmful to my
health.'

Now there is much in what the guy says, to be sure. I am
inclined to think, myself, that Dave will be somewhat disturbed
when he learns of this situation, especially when Miss Billy
Perry starts in being unhappy about it. But what is to be done I
do not know, except maybe to let the wedding go on, and then
when Waldo is out of reach of Dave, to put in a claim that he is
insane, and that the marriage does not count. It is a sure thing
I do not wish to be around when Dave the Dude hears Waldo
is already married.

I am thinking that maybe I better take it on the lam out of
here, when there is a great row at the door and I hear Dave the
Dude yelling that the preacher arrives. He is a very nice-looking
preacher, at that, though he seems somewhat surprised by the
goings-on, especially when Miss Missouri Martin steps up and
takes charge of him. Miss Missouri Martin tells him she is fond
of preachers, and is quite used to them, because she is twice
married by preachers, and twice by justices of the peace, and
once by a ship's captain at sea.

By this time one and all present, except maybe myself and
Waldo Winchester, and the preacher and maybe Miss Billy
Perry, are somewhat corned. Waldo is still sitting at his table

looking very sad and saying 'Yes' and 'No' to Miss Billy Perry whenever she skips past him, for Miss Billy Perry is too much pleasured up with happiness to stay long in one spot.

Dave the Dude is more corned than anybody else, because he has two or three days' running start on everybody. And when Dave the Dude is corned I wish to say that he is a very unreliable guy as to temper, and he is apt to explode right in your face any minute. But he seems to be getting a great bang out of the doings.

Well, by and by Nig Skolsky has the dance floor cleared, and then he moves out on the floor a sort of arch of very beautiful flowers. The idea seems to be that Miss Billy Perry and Waldo Winchester are to be married under this arch, I can see that Dave the Dude must put in several days planning this whole proposition, and it must cost him plenty of the old do-re-mi, especially as I see him showing Miss Missouri Martin a diamond ring as big as a cough drop.

'It is for the bride,' Dave the Dude says. 'The poor loogan she is marrying will never have enough dough to buy her such a rock, and she always wishes a big one. I get it off a guy who brings it in from Los Angeles. I am going to give the bride away myself in person, so how do I act, Mizzoo? I want Billy to have everything according to the book.'

Well, while Miss Missouri Martin is trying to remember back to one of her weddings to tell him, I take another peek at Waldo Winchester to see how he is making out. I once see two guys go to the old warm squativoo up in Sing Sing, and I wish to say both are laughing heartily compared to Waldo Winchester at this moment.

Miss Billy Perry is sitting with him and the orchestra leader is calling his men dirty names because none of them can think of how 'Oh, Promise Me' goes, when Dave the Dude yells: 'Well, we are all set! Let the happy couple step forward!'

Miss Billy Perry bounces up and grabs Waldo Winchester by the arm and pulls him up out of his chair. After a peek at his face I am willing to lay 6 to 5 he does not make the arch. But he finally gets there with everybody laughing and clapping their hands, and the preacher comes forward, and Dave the Dude looks happier than I ever see him look before in his life as they all get together under the arch of flowers.

Well, all of a sudden there is a terrible racket at the front door of the Woodcock Inn, with some doll doing a lot of hollering in a deep voice that sounds like a man's, and naturally everybody turns and looks that way. The doorman, a guy by the name of Slugsy Sachs, who is a very hard man indeed, seems to be trying to keep somebody out, but pretty soon there is a heavy bump and Slugsy Sachs falls down, and in comes a doll about four feet high and five feet wide.

In fact, I never see such a wide doll. She looks all hammered down. Her face is almost as wide as her shoulders, and makes me think of a great big full moon. She comes in bounding-like, and I can see that she is all churned up about something. As she bounces in, I hear a gurgle, and I look around to see Waldo Winchester slumping down to the floor, almost dragging Miss Billy Perry with him.

Well, the wide doll walks right up to the bunch under the arch and says in a large bass voice: 'Which one is Dave the Dude?'

'I am Dave the Dude,' says Dave the Dude, stepping up. 'What do you mean by busting in here like a walrus and gumming up our wedding?'

'So you are the guy who kidnaps my ever-loving husband to marry him off to this little red-headed pancake here, are you?' the wide doll says, looking at Dave the Dude, but pointing at Miss Billy Perry.

Well now, calling Miss Billy Perry a pancake to Dave the Dude is a very serious proposition, and Dave the Dude gets very angry. He is usually rather polite to dolls, but you can see he does not care for the wide doll's manner whatever.

'Say, listen here,' Dave the Dude says, 'you better take a walk before somebody clips you. You must be drunk,' he says. 'Or daffy,' he says. 'What are you talking about, anyway?'

'You will see what I am talking about,' the wide doll yells. 'The guy on the floor there is my lawful husband. You probably frighten him to death, the poor dear. You kidnap him to marry this red-headed thing, and I am going to get you arrested as sure as my name is Lola Sapola, you simple-looking tramp!'

Naturally, everybody is greatly horrified at a doll using such language to Dave the Dude, because Dave is known to shoot guys for much less, but instead of doing something to the wide doll at once, Dave says: 'What is this talk I hear? Who is married to who? Get out of here!' Dave says, grabbing the wide doll's arm.

Well, she makes out as if she is going to slap Dave in the face with her left hand, and Dave naturally pulls his kisser out of the way. But instead of doing anything with her left, Lola Sapola suddenly drives her right fist smack-dab into Dave the Dude's stomach, which naturally comes forward as his face goes back.

I wish to say I see many a body punch delivered in my life, but I never see a prettier one than this. What is more, Lola Sapola steps in with the punch, so there is plenty on it.

Now a guy who eats and drinks like Dave the Dude does cannot take them so good in the stomach, so Dave goes 'oof,' and sits down very hard on the dance floor, and as he is sitting there he is fumbling in his pants pocket for the old equalizer, so everybody around tears for cover except Lola Sapola, and Miss Billy Perry, and Waldo Winchester.

But before he can get his pistol out, Lola Sapola reaches down and grabs Dave by the collar and hoists him to his feet. She lets go her hold on him, leaving Dave standing on his pins, but teetering around somewhat, and then she drives her right hand to Dave's stomach a second time.

The punch drops Dave again, and Lola steps up to him as if she is going to give him the foot. But she only gathers up Waldo Winchester from off the floor and slings him across her shoulder like he is a sack of oats, and starts for the door. Dave the Dude sits up on the floor again and by this time he has the old equalizer in his duke.

'Only for me being a gentleman I will fill you full of slugs,' he yells.

Lola Sapola never even looks back, because by this time she

is petting Waldo Winchester's head and calling him loving names and saying what a shame it is for bad characters like Dave the Dude to be abusing her precious one. It all sounds to me as if Lola Sapola thinks well of Waldo Winchester.

Well, after she gets out of sight, Dave the Dude gets up off the floor and stands there looking at Miss Billy Perry, who is out to break all crying records. The rest of us come out from under cover, including the preacher, and we are wondering how mad Dave the Dude is going to be about the wedding being ruined. But Dave the Dude seems only disappointed and sad.

'Billy,' he says to Miss Billy Perry, 'I am mighty sorry you do not get your wedding. All I wish for is your happiness, but I do not believe you can ever be happy with this scribe if he also has to have his lion tamer around. As Cupid I am a total bust. This is the only nice thing I ever try to do in my whole life, and it is too bad it does not come off. Maybe if you wait until we can drown her, or something –'

'Dave,' says Miss Billy Perry, dropping so many tears that she seems to finally wash herself right into Dave the Dude's arms, 'I will never, never be happy with such a guy as Waldo Winchester. I can see now you are the only man for me.'

'Well, well, well,' Dave the Dude says, cheering right up. 'Where is the preacher? Bring on the preacher and let us have our wedding anyway.'

I see Mr and Mrs Dave the Dude the other day, and they seem very happy. But you never can tell about married people, so of course I am never going to let on to Dave the Dude that I am the one who telephones Lola Sapola at the Marx Hotel, because maybe I do not do Dave any too much of a favour, at that.

Neat Strip

Now this Rose Viola is twenty years old and is five feet five inches tall in her high-heeled shoes, and weighs one hundred and twenty pounds, net, and has a twenty-six waist, and a thirty-six bust, and wears a four and one-half shoe.

Moreover, she has a seven-inch ankle, and an eleven-inch calf, and the reason I know all these intimate details is because a friend of mine by the name of Rube Goldstein has Rose Viola in a burlesque show and advertises her as the American Venus, and he always prints these specifications in his ads.

But of course Rube Goldstein has no way of putting down in figures how beautiful Rose Viola is, because after all any pancake may have the same specifications and still be a rutabaga. All Rube can do is to show photographs of Rose Viola and after you see these photographs and then see Rose Viola herself you have half a mind to look the photographer up and ask him what he means by so grossly underestimating the situation.

She has big blue eyes, and hair the colour of sunup, and furthermore this colour is as natural as a six and five. Her skin is as white and as smooth as ivory and her teeth are like rows of new corn on the cob and she has a smile that starts slow and easy on her lips and in her eyes and seems to sort of flow over the rest of her face until any male characters observing same are wishing there is a murder handy that they can commit for her.

Well, I suppose by this time you are saying to yourself what is such a darberoo doing in a burlesque turkey, for burlesque is by no means an intellectual form of entertainment, and the answer to this question is that Rube Goldstein pays Rose Viola four hundred dollars per week, and this is by no means tin.

And the reason Rube Goldstein pays her such a sum is not because Rube is any philanthropist but because Rose Viola draws like a flaxseed poultice, for besides her looks she has that certain something that goes out across the footlights and hits every male character present smack-dab in the kisser and makes him hate to go home and gaze upon his ever-loving wife. In fact, I hear that for three weeks after Rose Viola plays a town the percentage of missing husbands appals the authorities.

It seems that the first time Rube Goldstein sees Rose Viola is in the city of Baltimore, Md., where his show is playing the old Gaiety, and one of Rube's chorus Judys, a sod widow who is with him nearly thirteen years and raises up three sons to manhood under him, runs off and marries a joskin from over on the eastern shore.

Naturally, Rube considers this a dirty trick, as he is so accustomed to seeing this Judy in his chorus that he feels his show will never look the same to him again; but the same night the widow is missing, Rose Viola appears before him asking for a situation.

Rube tells me he is greatly surprised at such a looking Judy seeking a place in a burlesque show and he explains to Rose Viola that it is a very tough life, to be sure, and that the pay is small, and that she will probably do better for herself if she gets a job dealing them off her arm in a beanery, or some such, but she requests Rube to kindly omit the alfalfa and give her a job, and Rube can see at once by the way she talks that she has personality.

So he hires her at twenty-five slugs per week to start with and raises her to half a C and makes her a principal the second night when he finds eighteen blokes lined up at the stage door after the show looking to date her up. In three weeks she is his star and he is three-sheeting her as if she is Katherine Cornell.

She comes out on the stage all dressed up in a beautiful evening gown and sings a little song, and as soon as she begins singing you wonder, unless you see her before, what she really is, as you can see by her voice that she is scarcely a singer by trade.

Her voice is not at all the same as Lily Pons's and in fact it is more like an old-fashioned coffee grinder, and about the time you commence to figure that she must be something like a magician and will soon start pulling rabbits out of a hat, Rose Viola begins to dance.

It is not a regular dance, to be sure. It is more of a hop and a skip and a jump back and forth across the stage, and as she is hopping and skipping and jumping, Rose Viola is also feeling around for zippers here and there about her person, and finally the evening gown disappears and she seems to be slightly dishabille but in a genteel manner, and then you can see by her shape that she is indeed a great artist.

Sometimes she will come down off the stage and work along the centre aisle, and this is when the audience really enjoys her most, as she will always stop before some bald-headed old character in an aisle seat where bald-headed characters are generally found, and will pretend to make a great fuss over him, singing to him, and maybe kissing him on top of the bald head and leaving the print of her lips in rouge there, which sometimes puts bald-headed characters to a lot of bother explaining when they get home.

She has a way of laughing and talking back to an audience and keeping it in good humour while she is working, although outside the theatre Rose Viola is very serious, and seldom has much to say. In fact, Rose Viola has so little to say that there are rumours in some quarters that she is a trifle dumb, but personally I would not mind being dumb myself at four hundred boffoes per week.

Well, it seems that a character by the name of Newsbaum, who runs a spot called the Pigeon Club, hears of Rose Viola, and he goes to see her one night at the old Mid Theatre on Broadway where Rube's show is playing a New York engagement, and this Newsbaum is such a character as is always looking for novelties for his club and he decides that Rose Viola will go good there.

So he offers her a chance to double at his club, working there after she gets through with her regular show, and Rube Goldstein advises her to take it, as Rube is very fond of Rose and he says this may be a first step upward in her career because the Pigeon Club is patronized only by very high-class rumpots.

So Rose Viola opens one night at the Pigeon Club, and she is working on the dance floor close to the tables, and doing the same act she does in burlesque, when a large young character who is sitting at one of the front tables with a bunch of other young characters, including several nice-looking Judys, reaches out and touches Rose Viola with the end of a cigarette in a spot she just unzippers.

Now of course this is all in a spirit of fun, but it is something that never happens in a burlesque house, and naturally Rose is startled no little, and quite some, and in addition to this she is greatly pained, as it seems that it is the lighted end of the cigarette that the large young character touches her with.

So she begins letting out screams, and these screams attract the attention of Rube Goldstein, who is present to see how she gets along at her opening, and although Rube is nearly seventy years old, and is fat and slow and sleepy-looking, he steps forward and flattens the large young character with a dish of chicken à la king, which he picks up off a nearby table.

Well, it seems that the large young character is nobody but a character by the name of Mr Choicer, who has great sums of money, and a fine social position, and this incident creates some little confusion, especially as old Rube Goldstein also flattens Newsbaum with another plate, this one containing lobster Newberg, when Newsbaum comes along complaining about Rube ruining his chinaware and also one of his best-paying customers.

Then Rube puts his arm around Rose Viola and makes her get dressed and leads her out of the Pigeon Club and up to Mindy's restaurant on Broadway, where I am personally present to observe much of what follows.

They sit down at my table and order up a couple of oyster stews, and Rose Viola is still crying at intervals, especially when she happens to rub the spot where the lighted cigarette hits, and Rube Goldstein is saying that for two cents he will go back to the Pigeon Club and flatten somebody again, when all of a sudden the door opens and in comes a young character in dinner clothes.

He is without a hat, and he is looking rumpled up no little, and on observing him, Rose Viola lets out a small cry, and Rube Goldstein picks up his bowl of oyster stew and starts getting to his feet, for it seems that they both recognize the young character as one of the characters at Mr Choicer's table in the Pigeon Club.

This young character rushes up in great excitement, and grabs Rube's arm before Rube can let fly with the oyster stew, and he holds Rube down in his chair, and looks at Rose Viola and speaks to her as follows:

'Oh,' he says, 'I search everywhere for you after you leave the Pigeon Club. I wish to beg your pardon for what happens there. I am ashamed of my friend Mr Choicer. I will never speak to him again as long as I live. He is a scoundrel. Furthermore, he is in bad shape from the chicken à la king. Oh,' the young character says, 'please forgive me for ever knowing him.'

Well, all the time he is talking, he is holding Rube Goldstein down and looking at Rose Viola, and she is looking back at him, and in five minutes more they do not know Rube Goldstein and me are in the restaurant, and in fact they are off by themselves at another table so the young character can make his apologies clearer, and Rube Goldstein is saying to me that after nearly seventy years he comes to the conclusion that the Judys never change.

So, then, this is the beginning of a wonderful romance, and in fact it is love at first sight on both sides, and very pleasant to behold, at that.

It seems that the name of the young character is Daniel Frame, and that he is twenty-six years of age, and in his last year in law school at Yale, and that he comes to New York for a weekend visit and runs into his old college chum, Mr Choicer, and now here he is in love.

I learn these details afterward from Rose Viola, and I also learn that this Daniel Frame is an only child, and lives with his widowed mother in a two-story white colonial house with ivy on the walls, and a yard around it, just outside the city of Manchester, N.H.

I learn that his mother has an old poodle dog by the name of Rags, and three servants, and that she lives very quietly, and never goes anywhere much except maybe to church and that the moonlight is something wonderful up around Manchester, N.H.

Furthermore, I learn that Daniel Frame comes of the best people in New England, and that he likes skiing, and Benny Goodman's band, and hates mufflers around his neck, and is very fond of popovers for breakfast, and that his eyes are dark brown, and that he is six feet even and weighs one hundred and eighty pounds and that he never goes to a dentist in his life.

I also learn that the ring he wears on the little finger of his left hand is his family crest, and that he sings baritone with a glee club, and the chances are I will learn plenty more about Daniel Frame if I care to listen any further to Rose Viola.

'He wishes to marry me,' Rose says. 'He wishes to take me to the white colonial house outside of Manchester, N.H., where we can raise Sealyham terriers, and maybe children. I love Sealyham terriers,' she says. 'They are awfully cute. Daniel wishes me to quit burlesque entirely. He sees me work at the Mid the other night and he thinks I am wonderful, but,' Rose says, 'he says it worries him constantly to think of me out there on that stage running the risk of catching colds.

'Another thing,' Rose Viola says, 'Daniel wishes me to meet his mother, but he is afraid she will be greatly horrified if she finds out the way I am exposed to the danger of catching colds. He says,' Rose says, 'that his mother is very strict about such things.'

Personally, I consider Daniel Frame a very wishy-washy sort of character, and by no means suitable to a strong personality such as Rose Viola, but when I ask Rube Goldstein what he thinks about it, Rube says to me like this:

'Well,' he says, 'I think it will be a fine thing for her to marry this young character, although,' Rube says, 'from what he tells her of his mother, I do not see how they are going to get past her. I know these old New England broads,' he says. 'They consider burlesque anything but a worthy amusement. Still,' he says, 'I have no kick coming about the male characters of New England. They are always excellent customers of mine.'

'Why,' I say, 'Rose Viola is a fine artist, and does not need such a thing as marriage.'

'Yes,' Rube says, 'she is the finest artist in her line I ever see but one. Laura Legayo is still tops with me. She retires on me away back yonder before you ever see one of my shows. But,' he says, 'if Rose marries this young character, she will have a home, and a future. Rose needs a future.

'This burlesque business is about done around here for a while,' Rube says. 'I can see the signs. The blats are beefing, and the cops are complaining about this and that, and one thing and another. They have no soul for art, and besides we are the easiest marks around when the reformers start rousing the cops for anything whatever.

'It is always this way with burlesque,' Rube says. 'It is up and down. It is on the way down now, and Rose may not still be young enough by the time it goes up again. Yes,' he says, 'Rose needs a future.'

Well, it seems that old Rube is a pretty good guesser, because a couple of nights later he gets an order from the police commissioner that there must be no more of this and that, and one thing and another, in his show, and what is more the police commissioner puts cops in all the burlesque houses to see that his order is obeyed.

At first Rube Goldstein figures that he may as well close down his New York run at once, and move to some city that is more hospitable to art, but he is wedged in at the Mid on a contract to pay rent for a few weeks longer, so while he is trying to think what is the best thing to do, he lets the show go on just the same, but omitting this and that, and one thing and another, so as not to offend the police commissioner in case he comes around looking for offence, or the cop the commissioner places on duty in the Mid, who is a character by the name of Halligan.

So there is Rose Viola out on the stage of the Mid doing her number in full costume without ever reaching for as much as a single zipper, and I can see what Rube Goldstein means when he says Rose needs a future, because looking at Rose in full costume really becomes quite monotonous after a while.

To tell the truth, the only one who seems to appreciate Rose in full costume is Daniel Frame when he comes down from Yale one weekend and finds her in this condition. In fact, Daniel Frame is really quite delighted with her.

'It is wonderful,' he says. 'It is especially wonderful because I tell my mother all about you, and she is talking of coming down from Manchester, N.H., to see you perform, and I have been worrying myself sick over her beholding you out there in danger of catching colds. I know she will be greatly pleased with you now, because,' he says, 'you look so sweet and modest and so well dressed.'

Naturally, as long as he is pleased, Rose Viola is pleased too, except that she suffers somewhat from the heat, for there is no doubt but what Rose is greatly in love with him and she scarcely ever talks about anything else, and does not seem to care if her art suffers from the change.

Now it comes on another Saturday night and I am backstage at the Mid talking to Rube Goldstein and he is telling me that he is greatly surprised to find business holding up so good. The house is packed to the doors, and I tell Rube that maybe he is wrong all these years and that the public appreciates art even when it has clothes on, but Rube says he thinks not. He says he thinks it is more likely that the customers are just naturally optimists.

Rose Viola is on the stage in full costume singing her song when all of a sudden somebody in the back of the audience lets out a yell of fire and this is an alarming cry in any theatre, to be sure, and especially in a spot like the Mid as it is an old house, and about as well fixed to stand off a fire as a barrel of grease. Then a duty fireman by the name of Rossoffsky, who is always on duty in the Mid when a show is on, comes rushing backstage and says it is a fire all right.

It seems that a cafeteria next door to the Mid is blazing inside and the flames are eating their way through the theatre wall at the front of the house by the main entrance, and in fact when the alarm is raised the whole wall is blazing on both sides, and it is a most disturbing situation, to be sure.

Well, the audience in the Mid is composed mostly of male characters, because male characters always appreciate burlesque much more than females or children, and these male characters now rise from their seats and start looking for the exits nearest to them, but by now they are shut off from the main entrance by the fire.

So they commence looking for other exits, and there are several of these, but it seems from what Rossoffsky says afterward that these exits are not used for so long that nobody figures it will ever be necessary to use them again, and the doors do not come open so easy, especially with so many trying to open them at once.

Then the male characters begin fighting with each other for the privilege of opening the doors, and also of getting out through the doors after they are opened, and this results in some confusion. In fact, it is not long before the male characters are fighting all over the premises, and knocking each other down, and stepping on each other's faces in a most discourteous manner.

While it is well known to one and all that a burlesque theatre is no place to take an ever-loving wife to begin with, it seems that some of these male characters have their wives with them, and these wives start screaming, but of course they are among the first knocked down and stepped on, so not much is heard of them until afterward.

A few of the male characters are smart enough to leap up on the stage and high-tail it out of there by the back way, but most of them are so busy fighting on the floor of the theatre that they do not think of this means of exit, and it is just as well that they do not think of it all at once, at that, as there is but one narrow stage door, and a rush will soon pile them up like jack-rabbits there.

The orchestra quits playing and the musicians are dropping their instruments and getting ready to duck under the stage and Rose Viola is standing still in the centre of the stage with her mouth open, looking this way and that in some astonishment and alarm, when all of a sudden a tall, stern-looking old Judy with white hair, and dressed in grey, stands up on a seat in the front row right back of the orchestra leader, and says to Rose Viola like this:

'Quick,' she says. 'Go into your routine.'

Well, Rose Viola still stands there as if she cannot figure out what the old Judy is talking about, and the old Judy makes motions at her with her hands, and then slowly unbuttons a little grey jacket she is wearing, and tosses it aside, and Rose gets the idea.

Now the stern-looking old Judy looks over to the orchestra leader, who is a character by the name of Butwell, and who is with Rube Goldstein's burlesque show since about the year one, and says to him:

'Hit 'er, Buttsy.'

Well, old Buttsy takes a look at her, and then he takes another look, and then he raises his hand, and his musicians settle back in their chairs, and as Buttsy lets his hand fall, they start playing Rose Viola's music, and the tall, stern-looking old Judy stands there on the seat in the front row pointing at the stage and hollering so loud her voice is heard above all the confusion of the male characters at their fighting.

'Look, boys,' she hollers.

And there on the stage is Rose Viola doing her hop, skip and a jump back and forth and feeling for the zippers here and there about her person, and finding same.

Now, on hearing the old Judy's voice, and on observing the scene on the stage, the customers gradually stop fighting with each other and begin easing themselves back into the seats, and paying strict attention to Rose Viola's performance, and all this time the wall behind them is blazing, and it is hotter than one hundred and six in the shade, and smoke is pouring into the Mid, and anybody will tell you that Rose Viola's feat of holding an audience against a house fire is really quite unsurpassed in theatrical history.

The tall, stern-looking old Judy remains standing on the seat in the front row until there are cries behind her to sit down, because it seems she is obstructing the view of some of those back of her, so finally she takes her seat, and Rose Viola keeps right on working.

By this time the fire department arrives and has the situation in the cafeteria under control, and the fire in the wall extinguished, and a fire captain and a squad of men come into the Mid, because it seems that rumours are abroad that a great catastrophe takes place in the theatre. In fact, the captain and his men are greatly alarmed because they cannot see a thing inside the Mid when they first enter on account of the smoke, and the captain sings out as follows:

'Is everybody dead in here?'

Then he sees through the smoke what is going on there on the stage, and he stops and begins enjoying the scene himself, and his men join him, and a good time is being had by one and all until all of a sudden Rose Viola keels over in a faint from her exertions. Rube orders the curtain down but the audience, including the firemen, remain for some time afterward in the theatre, hoping they may get an encore.

While I am standing near the stage door in readiness to take it on the Jesse Owens out of there in case the fire gets close, who comes running up all out of breath but Daniel Frame.

'I just get off the train from New Haven,' he says. 'I run all the way from the station on hearing a report that the Mid is on fire. Is anybody hurt?' he says. 'Is Rose safe?'

Well, I suggest that the best way to find out about this is to go inside and see, so we enter together, and there among the scenery we find Rube Goldstein and a bunch of actors still in their makeups gathered about Rose Viola, who is just getting to her feet and looking somewhat nonplussed.

At this same moment, Halligan, the cop stationed in the Mid, comes backstage, and pushes his way through the bunch around Rose Viola and taps her on the shoulder and says to her:

'You are under arrest,' Halligan says. 'I guess I will have to take you, too, Mr Goldstein,' he says.

'My goodness,' Daniel Frame says. 'What is Miss Viola under arrest for?'

'For putting on that number out there just now,' Halligan says. 'It's a violation of the police commissioner's order.'

'Heavens and earth,' Daniel Frame says. 'Rose, do not tell me you are out there tonight running the risk of catching cold, as before?'

'Yes,' Rose says.

'Oh, my goodness,' Daniel Frame says, 'and all the time my mother is sitting out there in the audience. I figure this week is a great time for her to see you perform, Rose,' he says. 'I cannot get down from New Haven in time to go with her, but I send her alone to see you, and I am to meet her after the theatre with you and introduce you to her. What will she think?'

'Well,' Halligan says, 'I have plenty of evidence against this party. In fact, I see her myself. Not bad,' he says. 'Not bad.'

Rose Viola is standing there looking at Daniel Frame in a sad way, and Daniel Frame is looking at Rose Viola in even a sadder way, when Rossoffsky, the fireman, shoves his way into the gathering, and says to Halligan:

'Copper,' he says, 'I overhear your remarks. Kindly take a

walk,' he says. 'If it is not for this party putting on that number out there, the chances are there will be a hundred dead in the aisles from the panic. In fact,' he says, 'I remember seeing you yourself knock over six guys trying to reach an exit before she starts dancing. She is a heroine,' he says. 'That is what she is, and I will testify to it in court.'

At this point who steps in through the stage door but the tall, stern-looking old Judy in grey, and when he sees her, Daniel Frame runs up to her and says:

'Oh, Mother,' he says, 'I am so mortified. Still,' he says, 'I love her just the same.'

But the old Judy scarcely notices him because by this time Rube Goldstein is shaking both of her hands and then over Rube's shoulder she sees Rose Viola, and she says to Rose like this:

'Well, miss,' she says, 'that is a right neat strip you do out there just now, although,' she says, 'you are mighty slow getting into it. You need polishing in spots, and then you will be okay. Rube,' she says, 'speaking of neat strips, who is the best you ever see?'

'Well,' Rube Goldstein says, 'if you are talking of the matter as art, I will say that thirty years ago, if they happen to be holding any competitions anywhere, I will be betting on you against the world, Laura.'

Dancing Dan's Christmas

Now one time it comes on Christmas, and in fact it is the evening before Christmas, and I am in Good Time Charley Bernstein's little speakeasy in West Forty-seventh Street, wishing Charley a Merry Christmas and having a few hot Tom and Jerrys with him.

This hot Tom and Jerry is an old-time drink that is once used by one and all in this country to celebrate Christmas with, and in fact it is once so popular that many people think Christmas is invented only to furnish an excuse for hot Tom and Jerry, although of course this is by no means true.

But anybody will tell you that there is nothing that brings out the true holiday spirit like hot Tom and Jerry, and I hear that since Tom and Jerry goes out of style in the United States, the holiday spirit is never quite the same.

The reason hot Tom and Jerry goes out of style is because it is necessary to use rum and one thing and another in making Tom and Jerry, and naturally when rum becomes illegal in this country Tom and Jerry is also against the law, because rum is something that is very hard to get around town these days.

For a while some people try making hot Tom and Jerry without putting rum in it, but somehow it never has the same old holiday spirit, so nearly everybody finally gives up in disgust, and this is not surprising, as making Tom and Jerry is by no means child's play. In fact, it takes quite an expert to make good Tom and Jerry, and in the days when it is not illegal a good hot Tom and Jerry maker commands good wages and many friends.

Now of course Good Time Charley and I are not using rum in the Tom and Jerry we are making, as we do not wish to do anything illegal. What we are using is rye whisky that Good Time Charley gets on a doctor's prescription from a drug store, as we are personally drinking this hot Tom and Jerry and naturally we are not foolish enough to use any of Good Time Charley's own rye in it.

The prescription for the rye whisky comes from old Doc Moggs, who prescribes it for Good Time Charley's rheumatism in case Charley happens to get any rheumatism, as Doc Moggs says there is nothing better for rheumatism than rye whisky, especially if it is made up in a hot Tom and Jerry. In fact, old Doc Moggs comes around and has a few seidels of hot Tom and Jerry with us for his own rheumatism.

He comes around during the afternoon, for Good Time Charley and I start making this Tom and Jerry early in the day, so as to be sure to have enough to last us over Christmas, and it is now along towards six o'clock, and our holiday spirit is practically one hundred per cent.

Well, as Good Time Charley and I are expressing our holiday sentiments to each other over our hot Tom and Jerry, and I am trying to think up the poem about the night before Christmas and all through the house, which I know will interest Charley no little, all of a sudden there is a big knock at the front door, and when Charley opens the door who comes in carrying a large package under one arm but a guy by the name of Dancing Dan.

This Dancing Dan is a good-looking young guy, who always seems well-dressed, and he is called by the name of Dancing Dan because he is a great hand for dancing around and about with dolls in night clubs, and other spots where there is any dancing. In fact, Dan never seems to be doing anything else, although I hear rumours that when he is not dancing he is carrying on in a most illegal manner at one thing and another. But of course you can always hear rumours in this town about anybody, and personally I am rather fond of Dancing Dan as he always seems to be getting a great belt out of life.

Anybody in town will tell you that Dancing Dan is a guy

with no Barnaby whatever in him, and in fact he has about as much gizzard as anybody around, although I wish to say I always question his judgement in dancing so much with Miss Muriel O'Neill, who works in the Half Moon night club. And the reason I question his judgement in this respect is because everybody knows that Miss Muriel O'Neill is a doll who is very well thought of by Heine Schmitz, and Heine Schmitz is not such a guy as will take kindly to anybody dancing more than once and a half with a doll that he thinks well of.

This Heine Schmitz is a very influential citizen of Harlem, where he has large interests in beer, and other business enterprises, and it is by no means violating any confidence to tell you that Heine Schmitz will just as soon blow your brains out as look at you. In fact, I hear sooner. Anyway, he is not a guy to monkey with and many citizens take the trouble to advise Dancing Dan that he is not only away out of line in dancing with Miss Muriel O'Neill, but that he is knocking his own price down to where he is no price at all.

But Dancing Dan only laughs ha-ha, and goes on dancing with Miss Muriel O'Neill any time he gets a chance, and Good Time Charley says he does not blame him, at that, as Miss Muriel O'Neill is so beautiful that he will be dancing with her himself no matter what, if he is five years younger and can get a Roscoe out as fast as in the days when he runs with Paddy the Link and other fast guys.

Well, anyway, as Dancing Dan comes in he weighs up the joint in one quick peek, and then he tosses the package he is carrying into a corner where it goes plunk, as if there is something very heavy in it, and then he steps up to the bar alongside of Charley and me and wishes to know what we are drinking.

Naturally we start boosting hot Tom and Jerry to Dancing Dan, and he says he will take a crack at it with us, and after one crack, Dancing Dan says he will have another crack, and Merry Christmas to us with it, and the first thing anybody knows it is a couple of hours later and we are still having cracks at the hot

Tom and Jerry with Dancing Dan, and Dan says he never drinks anything so soothing in his life. In fact, Dancing Dan says he will recommend Tom and Jerry to everybody he knows, only he does not know anybody good enough for Tom and Jerry, except maybe Miss Muriel O'Neill, and she does not drink anything with drugstore rye in it.

Well, several times while we are drinking this Tom and Jerry, customers come to the door of Good Time Charley's little speakeasy and knock, but by now Charley is commencing to be afraid they will wish Tom and Jerry, too, and he does not feel we will have enough for ourselves, so he hangs out a sign which says 'Closed on Account of Christmas', and the only one he will let in is a guy by the name of Ooky, who is nothing but an old rum-dum, and who is going around all week dressed like Santa Claus and carrying a sign advertising Moe Lewinsky's clothing joint around in Sixth Avenue.

This Ooky is still wearing his Santa Claus outfit when Charley lets him in, and the reason Charley permits such a character as Ooky in his joint is because Ooky does the porter work for Charley when he is not Santa Claus for Moe Lewinsky, such as sweeping out, and washing the glasses, and one thing and another.

Well, it is about nine-thirty when Ooky comes in, and his puppies are aching, and he is all petered out generally from walking up and down and here and there with his sign, for any time a guy is Santa Claus for Moe Lewinsky he must earn his dough. In fact, Ooky is so fatigued, and his puppies hurt him so much, that Dancing Dan and Good Time Charley and I all feel very sorry for him, and invite him to have a few mugs of hot Tom and Jerry with us, and wish him plenty of Merry Christmas.

But old Ooky is not accustomed to Tom and Jerry, and after about the fifth mug he folds up in a chair, and goes right to sleep on us. He is wearing a pretty good Santa Claus make-up, what with a nice red suit trimmed with white cotton, and a wig, and false nose, and long white whiskers, and a big sack stuffed with excelsior on his back, and if I do not know Santa Claus is not apt to be such a guy as will snore loud enough to rattle the windows, I will think Ooky is Santa Claus sure enough.

Well, we forget Ooky and let him sleep, and go on with our hot Tom and Jerry, and in the meantime we try to think up a few songs appropriate to Christmas, and Dancing Dan finally renders My Dad's Dinner Pail in a nice baritone and very loud, while I do first-rate with Will You Love Me in December – As You Do in May? But personally I always think Good Time Charley Bernstein is a little out of line trying to sing a hymn in Jewish on such an occasion, and it causes words between us.

While we are singing many customers come to the door and knock, and then they read Charley's sign, and this seems to cause some unrest among them, and some of them stand outside saying it is a great outrage, until Charley sticks his noggin out the door and threatens to bust somebody's beezer if they do not go on about their business and stop disturbing peaceful citizens.

Naturally the customers go away, as they do not wish their beezers busted, and Dancing Dan and Charley and I continue drinking our hot Tom and Jerry, and with each Tom and Jerry we are wishing one another a very Merry Christmas, and sometimes a very Happy New Year, although of course this does not go for Good Time Charley as yet, because Charley has his New Year separate from Dancing Dan and me.

By and by we take to waking Ooky up in his Santa Claus outfit and offering him more hot Tom and Jerry, and wishing him Merry Christmas, but Ooky only gets sore and calls us names, so we can see he does not have the right holiday spirit in him, and let him alone until along about midnight when Dancing Dan wishes to see how he looks as Santa Claus.

So Good Time Charley and I help Dancing Dan pull off Ooky's outfit and put it on Dan, and this is easy as Ooky only has this Santa Claus outfit on over his ordinary clothes, and he does not even wake up when we are undressing him of the Santa Claus uniform.

Well, I wish to say I see many a Santa Claus in my time, but
I never see a better-looking Santa Claus than Dancing Dan,
especially after he gets the wig and white whiskers fixed just
right, and we put a sofa pillow that Good Time Charley
happens to have around the joint for the cat to sleep on down
his pants to give Dancing Dan a nice fat stomach such as Santa
Claus is bound to have.

In fact, after Dancing Dan looks at himself in a mirror
awhile he is greatly pleased with his appearance, while Good
Time Charley is practically hysterical, although personally I
am commencing to resent Charley's interest in Santa Claus,
and Christmas generally, as he by no means has any claim on
these matters. But then I remember Charley furnishes the hot
Tom and Jerry, so I am more tolerant towards him.

'Well,' Charley finally says, 'it is a great pity we do not know
where there are some stockings hung up somewhere, because
then,' he says, 'you can go around and stuff things in these
stockings, as I always hear this is the main idea of a Santa
Claus. But,' Charley says, 'I do not suppose anybody in this
section has any stockings hung up, or if they have,' he says,
'the chances are they are so full of holes they will not hold
anything. Anyway,' Charley says, 'even if there are any stockings hung up we do not have anything to stuff in them,
although personally,' he says, 'I will gladly donate a few pints
of Scotch.'

Well, I am pointing out that we have no reindeer and that a
Santa Claus is bound to look like a terrible sap if he goes
around without any reindeer, but Charley's remarks seem to
give Dancing Dan an idea, for all of a sudden he speaks as
follows:

'Why,' Dancing Dan says, 'I know where a stocking is hung
up. It is hung up at Miss Muriel O'Neill's flat over here in
West Forty-ninth Street. This stocking is hung up by nobody
but a party by the name of Gammer O'Neill, who is Miss
Muriel O'Neill's grandmamma,' Dancing Dan says. 'Gammer
O'Neill is going on ninety-odd,' he says, 'and Miss Muriel

O'Neill tells me she cannot hold out much longer, what with one thing and another, including being a little childish in spots.

'Now,' Dancing Dan says, 'I remember Miss Muriel O'Neill is telling me just the other night how Gammer O'Neill hangs up her stocking on Christmas Eve all her life, and,' he says, 'I judge from what Miss Muriel O'Neill says that the old doll always believes Santa Claus will come along some Christmas and fill the stocking full of beautiful gifts. But,' Dancing Dan says, 'Miss Muriel O'Neill tells me Santa Claus never does this, although Miss Muriel O'Neill personally always takes a few gifts home and pops them into the stocking to make Gammer O'Neill feel better.

'But, of course,' Dancing Dan says, 'these gifts are nothing much because Miss Muriel O'Neill is very poor, and proud, and also good, and will not take a dime off of anybody, and I can lick the guy who says she will, although,' Dancing Dan says, 'between me, and Heine Schmitz, and a raft of other guys I can mention, Miss Muriel O'Neill can take plenty.'

Well, I know that what Dancing Dan states about Miss Muriel O'Neill is quite true, and in fact it is a matter that is often discussed on Broadway, because Miss Muriel O'Neill cannot get more than twenty bobs per week working in the Half Moon, and it is well known to one and all that this is no kind of dough for a doll as beautiful as Miss Muriel O'Neill.

'Now,' Dancing Dan goes on, 'it seems that while Gammer O'Neill is very happy to get whatever she finds in her stocking on Christmas morning, she does not understand why Santa Claus is not more liberal, and,' he says, 'Miss Muriel O'Neill is saying to me that she only wishes she can give Gammer O'Neill one real big Christmas before the old doll puts her checks back in the rack.

'So,' Dancing Dan states, 'here is a job for us. Miss Muriel O'Neill and her grandmamma live all alone in this flat over in West Forty-ninth Street, and,' he says, 'at such an hour as this Miss Muriel O'Neill is bound to be working, and the chances are Gammer O'Neill is sound asleep, and we will just hop over there and Santa Claus will fill up her stocking with beautiful gifts.'

Well, I say, I do not see where we are going to get any beautiful gifts at this time of night, what with all the stores being closed, unless we dash into an all-night drug store and buy a few bottles of perfume and a bum toilet set as guys always do when they forget about their ever-loving wives until after store hours on Christmas Eve, but Dancing Dan says never mind about this, but let us have a few more Tom and Jerrys first.

So we have a few more Tom and Jerrys, and then Dancing Dan picks up the package he heaves into the corner, and dumps most of the excelsior out of Ooky's Santa Claus sack, and puts the bundle in, and Good Time Charley turns out all the lights but one, and leaves a bottle of Scotch on the table in front of Ooky for a Christmas gift, and away we go.

Personally, I regret very much leaving the hot Tom and Jerry, but then I am also very enthusiastic about going along to help Dancing Dan play Santa Claus, while Good Time Charley is practically overjoyed, as it is the first time in his life Charley is ever mixed up in so much holiday spirit. In fact, nothing will do Charley but that we stop in a couple of spots and have a few drinks to Santa Claus's health, and these visits are a big success, although everybody is much surprised to see Charley and me with Santa Claus, especially Charley, although nobody recognizes Dancing Dan.

But of course there are no hot Tom and Jerrys in these spots we visit, and we have to drink whatever is on hand, and personally I will always believe that the noggin I have on me afterwards comes of mixing the drinks we get in these spots with my Tom and Jerry.

As we go up Broadway, headed for Forty-ninth Street, Charley and I see many citizens we know and give them a large hello, and wish them Merry Christmas, and some of these citizens shake hands with Santa Claus, not knowing he is nobody but Dancing Dan, although later I understand there is some gossip among these citizens because they claim a Santa Claus with such a breath on him as our Santa Claus has is a little out of line.

And once we are somewhat embarrassed when a lot of little kids going home with their parents from a late Christmas party somewhere gather about Santa Claus with shouts of childish glee, and some of them wish to climb up Santa Claus's legs. Naturally, Santa Claus gets a little peevish, and calls them a few names, and one of the parents comes up and wishes to know what is the idea of Santa Claus using such language, and Santa Claus takes a punch at the parent, all of which is no doubt most astonishing to the little kids who have an idea of Santa Claus as a very kindly old guy. But of course they do not know about Dancing Dan mixing the liquor we get in the spots we visit with his Tom and Jerry, or they will understand how even Santa Claus can lose his temper.

Well, finally we arrive in front of the place where Dancing Dan says Miss Muriel O'Neill and her grandmamma live, and it is nothing but a tenement house not far back of Madison Square Garden, and furthermore it is a walk-up, and at this time there are no lights burning in the joint except a gas jet in the main hall, and by the light of this jet we look at the names on the letter-boxes, such as you always find in the hall of these joints, and we see that Miss Muriel O'Neill and her grand-mamma live on the fifth floor.

This is the top floor, and personally I do not like the idea of walking up five flights of stairs, and I am willing to let Dancing Dan and Good Time Charley go, but Dancing Dan insists we must all go, and finally I agree because Charley is commencing to argue that the right way for us to do is to get on the roof and let Santa Claus go down a chimney, and is making so much noise I am afraid he will wake somebody up.

So up the stairs we climb and finally we come to a door on the top floor that has a little card in a slot that says O'Neill, so we know we reach our destination. Dancing Dan first tries the knob, and right away the door opens, and we are in a little two- or three-room flat, with not much furniture in it, and what furniture there is is very poor. One single gas jet is burning near a bed in a room just off the one the door opens into, and by this light we see a very old doll is sleeping on the bed, so we judge this is nobody but Gammer O'Neill.

On her face is a large smile, as if she is dreaming of something very pleasant. On a chair at the head of the bed is hung a long black stocking, and it seems to be such a stocking as is often patched and mended, so I can see what Miss Muriel O'Neill tells Dancing Dan about her grandmamma hanging up her stocking is really true, although up to this time I have my doubts.

Well, I am willing to pack in after one gander at the old doll, especially as Good Time Charley is commencing to prowl around the flat to see if there is a chimney where Santa Claus can come down, and is knocking things over, but Dancing Dan stands looking down at Gammer O'Neil for a long time.

Finally he unslings the sack on his back, and takes out his package, and unties this package, and all of a sudden out pops a raft of big diamond bracelets, and diamond rings, and diamond brooches, and diamond necklaces, and I do not know what all else in the way of diamonds, and Dancing Dan and I begin stuffing these diamonds into the stocking and Good Time Charley pitches in and helps us.

There are enough diamonds to fill the stocking to the muzzle, and it is no small stocking, at that, and I judge that Gammer O'Neill has a pretty fair set of bunting sticks when she is young. In fact, there are so many diamonds that we have enough left over to make a nice little pile on the chair after we fill the stocking plumb up, leaving a nice diamond-studded vanity case sticking out the top where we figure it will hit Gammer O'Neill's eye when she wakes up.

And it is not until I get out in the fresh air again that all of a sudden I remember seeing large headlines in the afternoon papers about a five-hundred-G's stick-up in the afternoon of one of the biggest diamond merchants in Maiden Lane while he is sitting in his office, and I also recall once hearing rumours that Dancing Dan is one of the best lone-hand git-'em-up guys in the world.

Naturally I commence to wonder if I am in the proper company when I am with Dancing Dan, even if he is Santa Claus. So I leave him on the next corner arguing with Good Time Charley about whether they ought to go and find some more presents somewhere, and look for other stockings to stuff, and I hasten on home, and go to bed.

. The next day I find I have such a noggin that I do not care to stir around, and in fact I do not stir around much for a couple of weeks.

Then one night I drop around to Good Time Charley's little speakeasy, and ask Charley what is doing.

'Well,' Charley says, 'many things are doing, and personally,' he says, 'I am greatly surprised I do not see you at Gammer O'Neill's wake. You know Gammer O'Neill leaves this wicked old world a couple of days after Christmas,' Good Time Charley says, 'and,' he says, 'Miss Muriel O'Neill states that Doc Moggs claims it is at least a day after she is entitled to go, but she is sustained,' Charley says, 'by great happiness on finding her stocking filled with beautiful gifts on Christmas morning.

'According to Miss Muriel O'Neill,' Charley says, 'Gammer O'Neill dies practically convinced that there is a Santa Claus, although of course,' he says, 'Miss Muriel O'Neill does not tell her the real owner of the gifts, an all-right guy by the name of Shapiro, leaves the gifts with her after Miss Muriel O'Neill notifies him of the finding of same.

'It seems,' Charley says, 'this Shapiro is a tender-hearted guy, who is willing to help keep Gammer O'Neill with us a little longer when Doc Moggs says leaving the gifts with her will do it.

'So,' Charley says, 'everything is quite all right, as the coppers cannot figure anything except that maybe the rascal who takes the gifts from Shapiro gets conscience stricken, and leaves them the first place he can, and Miss Muriel O'Neill

receives a ten-G's reward for finding the gifts and returning
them. And,' Charley says, 'I hear Dancing Dan is in San
Francisco and is figuring on reforming and becoming a dancing
teacher, so he can marry Miss Muriel O'Neill, and of course,'
he says, 'we all hope and trust she never learns any details of
Dancing Dan's career.'

Well, it is Christmas Eve a year later that I run into a guy by
the name of Shotgun Sam, who is mobbed up with Heine
Schmitz in Harlem, and who is a very, very obnoxious character
indeed.

'Well, well, well,' Shotgun says, 'the last time I see you is
another Christmas Eve like this, and you are coming out of
Good Time Charley's joint, and,' he says, 'you certainly have
your pots on.'

'Well, Shotgun,' I say, 'I am sorry you get such a wrong
impression of me, but the truth is,' I say, 'on the occasion you
speak of, I am suffering from a dizzy feeling in my head.'

'It is all right with me,' Shotgun says. 'I have a tip this guy
Dancing Dan is in Good Time Charley's the night I see you,
and Mockie Morgan and Gunner Jack and me are casing the
joint, because,' he says, 'Heine Schmitz is all sored up at Dan
over some doll, although of course,' Shotgun says, 'it is all
right now, as Heine has another doll.

'Anyway,' he says, 'we never get to see Dancing Dan. We
watch the joint from six-thirty in the evening until daylight
Christmas morning, and nobody goes in all night but old Ooky
the Santa Claus guy in his Santa Claus make-up, and,' Shotgun
says, 'nobody comes out except you and Good Time Charley
and Ooky.

'Well,' Shotgun says, 'it is a great break for Dancing Dan he
never goes in or comes out of Good Time Charley's, at that,
because,' he says, 'we are waiting for him on the second-floor
front of the building across the way with some nice little
sawed-offs, and are under orders from Heine not to miss.'

'Well, Shotgun,' I say, 'Merry Christmas.'

'Well, all right,' Shotgun says, 'Merry Christmas.'

Tobias the Terrible

One night I am sitting in Mindy's restaurant on Broadway partaking heartily of some Hungarian goulash which comes very nice in Mindy's, what with the chef being personally somewhat Hungarian himself, when in pops a guy who is a stranger to me and sits down at my table.

I do not pay any attention to the guy at first as I am busy looking over the entries for the next day at Laurel, but I hear him tell the waiter to bring him some goulash, too. By and by I hear the guy making a strange noise and I look at him over my paper and see that he is crying. In fact, large tears are rolling down his face into his goulash and going plop-plop as they fall.

Now it is by no means usual to see guys crying in Mindy's restaurant, though thousands of guys come in there who often feel like crying, especially after a tough day at the track, so I commence weighing the guy up with great interest. I can see he is a very little guy, maybe a shade over five feet high and weighing maybe as much as a dime's worth of liver, and he has a moustache like a mosquito's whiskers across his upper lip, and pale blond hair and a very sad look in his eyes.

Furthermore, he is a young guy and he is wearing a suit of clothes the colour of French mustard, with slanting pockets, and I notice when he comes in that he has a brown hat sitting jack-deuce on his noggin. Anybody can see that this guy does not belong in these parts, with such a sad look and especially with such a hat.

Naturally, I figure his crying is some kind of a dodge. In fact, I figure that maybe the guy is trying to cry me out of the price of his Hungarian goulash, although if he takes the trouble to ask anybody before he comes in, he will learn that he may just as well try to cry Al Smith out of the Empire State Building.

But the guy does not say anything whatever to me but just goes on shedding tears into his goulash, and finally I get very curious about this proposition, and I speak to him as follows:

'Listen, pally,' I say, 'if you are crying about the goulash, you better dry your tears before the chef sees you, because,' I say, 'the chef is very sensitive about his goulash, and may take your tears as criticism.'

'The goulash seems all right,' the guy says in a voice that is just about his size. 'Anyway, I am not crying about the goulash. I am crying about my sad life. Friend,' the guy says, 'are you ever in love?'

Well, of course, at this crack I know what is eating the guy. If I have all the tears that are shed on Broadway by guys in love, I will have enough salt water to start an opposition ocean to the Atlantic and Pacific, with enough left over to run the Great Salt Lake out of business. But I wish to say I never shed any of these tears personally, because I am never in love, and furthermore, barring a bad break, I never expect to be in love, for the way I look at it love is strictly the old phedinkus, and I tell the little guy as much.

'Well,' he says, 'you will not speak so harshly of love if you are acquainted with Miss Deborah Weems.'

With this he starts crying more than somewhat, and his grief is such that it touches my heart and I have half a notion to start crying with him as I am now convinced that the guy is levelling with his tears.

Finally the guy slacks up a little in his crying, and begins eating his goulash, and by and by he seems more cheerful, but then it is well known to one and all that a fair dose of Mindy's goulash will cheer up anybody no matter how sad they feel. Pretty soon the guy starts talking to me, and I make out that his name is Tobias Tweeney, and that he comes from a spot over in Bucks County, Pennsylvania, by the name of Erasmus, or some such.

Furthermore, I judge that this Erasmus is not such a large city, but very pleasant, and that Tobias Tweeney is born and raised there and is never much of any place else in his life, although he is now rising twenty-five.

Well, it seems that Tobias Tweeney has a fine position in a shoe store selling shoes and is going along all right when he happens to fall in love with a doll by the name of Miss Deborah Weems, whose papa owns a gas station in Erasmus and is a very prominent citizen. I judge from what Tobias tells me that this Miss Deborah Weems tosses him around quite some, which proves to me that dolls in small towns are just the same as they are on Broadway.

'She is beautiful,' Tobias Tweeney says, speaking of Miss Deborah Weems. 'I do not think I can live without her. But,' he says, 'Miss Deborah Weems will have no part of me because she is daffy over desperate characters of the underworld such as she sees in the movies at the Model Theatre in Erasmus.

'She wishes to know,' Tobias Tweeney says, 'why I cannot be a big gunman and go around plugging people here and there and talking up to politicians and policemen, and maybe looking picturesque and romantic like Edward G. Robinson or James Cagney or even Georgie Raft. But, of course,' Tobias says, 'I am not the type for such a character. Anyway,' he says, 'Constable Wendell will never permit me to be such a character in Erasmus.

'So Miss Deborah Weems says I have no more nerve than a catfish,' Tobias says, 'and she goes around with a guy by the name of Joe Trivett, who runs the Smoke Shop, and bootlegs ginger extract to the boys in his back room and claims Al Capone once says "Hello" to him, although,' Tobias says, 'personally, I think Joe Trivett is nothing but a great big liar.'

At this, Tobias Tweeney starts crying again, and I feel very sorry for him indeed, because I can see he is a friendly, harmless little fellow, and by no means accustomed to being tossed around by a doll, and a guy who is not accustomed to being tossed around by a doll always finds it most painful the first time.

'Why,' I say, very indignant, 'this Miss Deborah Weems talks great foolishness, because big gunmen always wind up nowadays with the score nine to nought against them, even in the movies. In fact,' I say, 'if they do not wind up this way in the movies, the censors will not permit the movies to be displayed. Why do you not hit this guy Trivett a punch in the snoot,' I say, 'and tell him to go on about his business?'

'Well,' Tobias says, 'the reason I do not hit him a punch in the snoot is because he has the idea of punching snoots first, and whose snoot does he punch but mine. Furthermore,' Tobias says, 'he makes my snoot bleed with the punch, and he says he will do it again if I keep hanging around Miss Deborah Weems. And,' Tobias says, 'it is mainly because I do not return the punch, being too busy stopping my snoot from bleeding, that Miss Deborah Weems renounces me for ever.

'She says she can never stand for a guy who has no more nerve than me,' Tobias says, 'but,' he says, 'I ask you if I am to blame if my mother is frightened by a rabbit a few weeks before I am born, and marks me for life?

'So I leave town,' Tobias says. 'I take my savings of two hundred dollars out of the Erasmus bank, and I come here, figuring maybe I will meet up with some big gunmen and other desperate characters of the underworld, and get to know them, and then I can go back to Erasmus and make Joe Trivett look sick. By the way,' he says, 'do you know any desperate characters of the underworld?'

Well, of course I do not know any such characters, and if I do know them I am not going to speak about it, because the best a guy can get in this town if he goes around speaking of these matters is a nice kick in the pants. So I say no to Tobias Tweeney, and tell him I am more or less of a stranger myself, and then he wishes to know if I can show him a tough joint, such as he sees in the movies.

Naturally, I do not know of such a joint, but then I get to thinking about Good Time Charley's little Gingham Shoppe over in Forty-seventh Street, and how Charley is not going so good the last time I am in there, and here is maybe a chance for me to steer a little trade his way, because, after all, guys with two yards in their pocket are by no means common nowadays.

So I take Tobias Tweeney around to Good Time Charley's, but the moment we get in there I am sorry we go, because who is present but a dozen parties from different parts of the city, and none of these parties are any bargain at any time. Some of these parties, such as Harry the Horse and Angie the Ox, are from Brooklyn, and three are from Harlem, including Little Mitzi and Germany Schwartz, and several are from the Bronx, because I recognize Joey Uptown, and Joey never goes around without a few intimate friends from his own neighbourhood with him.

Afterwards I learn that these parties are to a meeting on business matters at a spot near Good Time Charley's, and when they get through with their business they drop in to give Charley a little complimentary play, for Charley stands very good with one and all in this town. Anyway, they are sitting around a table when Tobias Tweeney and I arrive, and I give them all a big hello, and they hello me back, and ask me and my friend to sit down as it seems they are in a most hospitable frame of mind.

Naturally I sit down because it is never good policy to decline an invitation from parties such as these, and I motion Tobias to sit down, too, and I introduce Tobias all around, and we all have a couple of drinks, and then I explain to those present just who Tobias is, and how his ever-loving doll tosses him around, and how Joe Trivett punches him in the snoot.

Well, Tobias begins crying again, because no inexperienced guy can take a couple of drinks of Good Time Charley's liquor and not bust out crying, even if it is Charley's company liquor, and one and all are at once very sympathetic with Tobias, especially Little Mitzi, who is just tossed around himself more than somewhat by a doll. In fact, Little Mitzi starts crying with him.

'Why,' Joey Uptown says, 'I never hear of a greater outrage

in my life, although,' he says, 'I can see there is some puppy in you at that, when you do not return this Trivett's punch. But even so,' Joey says, 'if I have time I will go back to this town you speak of with you and make the guy hard to catch. Furthermore,' he says, 'I will give this Miss Deborah Weems a piece of my mind.'

Then I tell them how Tobias Tweeney comes to New York figuring he may meet up with some desperate characters of the underworld, and they hear this with great interest, and Angie the Ox speaks as follows:

'I wonder,' Angie says, 'if we can get in touch with anybody who knows such characters and arrange to have Mr Tweeney meet them, although personally,' Angie says, 'I loathe and despise characters of this nature.'

Well, while Angie is wondering this there comes a large knock at the front door, and it is such a knock as only the gendarmes can knock, and everybody at the table jumps up. Good Time Charley goes to the door and takes a quiet gander through his peephole and we hear a loud, coarse voice speaking as follows:

'Open up, Charley,' the voice says. 'We wish to look over your guests. Furthermore,' the voice says, 'tell them not to try the back door, because we are there, too.'

'It is Lieutenant Harrigan and his squad,' Charley says as he comes back to the table where we are all standing. 'Someone must tip him off you are here. Well,' Charley says, 'those who have rods to shed will shed them now.'

At this, Joey Uptown steps up to Tobias Tweeney and hands him a large Betsy and says to Tobias like this:

'Put this away on you somewhere,' Joey says, 'and then sit down and be quiet. These coppers are not apt to bother with you,' Joey says, 'if you sit still and mind your own business, but,' Joey says, 'it will be very tough on any of us they find with a rod, especially any of us who owe the state any time, and,' Joey says, 'I seem to remember I owe some.'

Now of course what Joey says is very true, because he is only walking around and about on parole, and some of the others present are walking around the same way, and it is a very serious matter for a guy who is walking around on parole to be caught with a John Roscoe in his pocket. So it is a very ticklish situation, and somewhat embarrassing.

Well, Tobias Tweeney is somewhat dazed by his couple of drinks of Good Time Charley's liquor and the chances are he does not realize what is coming off, so he takes Joey's rod and puts it in his hip kick. Then all of a sudden Harry the Horse and Angie the Ox and Little Mitzi, and all the others step up to him and hand him their Roscoes and Tobias Tweeney somehow manages to stow the guns away on himself and sit down before Good Time Charley opens the door and in come the gendarmes.

By this time Joey Uptown and all the others are scattered at different tables around the room, with no more than three at any one table, leaving Tobias Tweeney and me alone at the table where we are first sitting. Furthermore, everybody is looking very innocent indeed, and all hands seem somewhat surprised at the intrusion of the gendarmes, who are all young guys belonging to Harrigan's Broadway squad, and very rude.

I know Harrigan by sight, and I know most of his men, and they know there is no more harm in me than there is in a two-year-old baby, so they pay no attention to me whatever, or to Tobias Tweeney, either, but go around making Joey Uptown, and Angie the Ox, and all the others stand up while the gendarmes fan them to see if they have any rods on them, because these gendarmes are always laying for parties such as these hoping to catch them rodded up.

Naturally the gendarmes do not find any rods on anybody, because the rods are all on Tobias Tweeney, and no gendarme is going to fan Tobias Tweeney looking for a rod after one gander at Tobias, especially at this particular moment, as Tobias is now half-asleep from Good Time Charley's liquor, and has no interest whatever in anything that is going on. In fact, Tobias is nodding in his chair.

Of course the gendarmes are greatly disgusted at not finding any rods, and Angie the Ox and Joey Uptown are telling them that they are going to see their aldermen and find out if law-abiding citizens can be stood up and fanned for rods, and put in a very undignified position like this, but the gendarmes do not seem disturbed by these threats, and Lieutenant Harrigan states as follows:

'Well,' he says, 'I guess maybe I get a bum steer, but,' he says, 'for two cents I will give all you wrong gees a good going-over just for luck.'

Of course this is no way to speak to parties such as these, as they are all very prominent in their different parts of the city, but Lieutenant Harrigan is a guy who seldom cares how he talks to anybody. In fact, Lieutenant Harrigan is a very tough copper.

But he is just about to take his gendarmes out of the joint when Tobias Tweeney nods a little too far forward in his chair, and then all of a sudden topples over on the floor, and five large rods pop out of his pockets and go sliding every which way around the floor, and the next thing anybody knows there is Tobias Tweeney under arrest with all the gendarmes holding on to some part of him.

Well, the next day the newspapers are plumb full of the capture of a guy they call Twelve-Gun Tweeney, and the papers say the police state that this is undoubtedly the toughest guy the world ever sees, because while they hear of two-gun guys, and even three-gun guys, they never before hear of a guy going around rodded up with twelve guns.

The gendarmes say they can tell by the way he acts that Twelve-Gun Tweeney is a mighty bloodthirsty guy, because he says nothing whatever but only glares at them with a steely glint in his eyes, although of course the reason Tobias stares at them is because he is still too dumbfounded to think of anything to say.

Naturally, I figure that when Tobias comes up for air he is a sure thing to spill the whole business, and all the parties who are in Good Time Charley's when he is arrested figure the same way, and go into retirement for a time. But it seems that when Tobias finally realizes what time it is, he is getting so much attention that it swells him all up and he decides to keep on being Twelve-Gun Tweeney as long as he can, which is a decision that is a very nice break for all parties concerned.

I sneak down to Judge Rascover's court the day Tobias is arraigned on a charge of violation of the Sullivan law, which is a law against carrying rods, and the courtroom is packed with citizens eager to see a character desperate enough to lug twelve rods, and among these citizens are many dolls, pulling and hauling for position, and some of these dolls are by no means crows. Many photographers are hanging around to take pictures of Twelve-Gun Tweeney as he is led in handcuffed to gendarmes on either side of him, and with other gendarmes in front and behind him.

But one and all are greatly surprised and somewhat disappointed when they see what a little squirt Tobias is, and Judge Rascover looks down at him once, and then puts on his specs and takes another gander as if he does not believe what he sees in the first place. After looking at Tobias awhile through his specs, and shaking his head as if he is greatly puzzled, Judge Rascover speaks to Lieutenant Harrigan as follows:

'Do you mean to tell this court,' Judge Rascover says, 'that this half-portion here is the desperate Twelve-Gun Tweeney?'

Well, Lieutenant Harrigan says there is no doubt whatever about it, and Judge Rascover wishes to know how Tobias carries all these rods, and whereabouts, so Lieutenant Harrigan collects twelve rods from the gendarmes around the courtroom, unloads these rods, and starts in putting the guns here and there on Tobias as near as he can remember where they are found on him in the first place, with Tobias giving him a little friendly assistance.

Lieutenant Harrigan puts two guns in each of the side pockets of Tobias's coat, one in each hip pocket, one in the waistband of Tobias's pants, one in each side pocket of the pants, one up each of Tobias's sleeves, and one in the inside pocket of Tobias's coat. Then Lieutenant Harrigan states to the court that he is all finished, and that Tobias is rodded up in every respect as when they put the arm on him in Good Time Charley's joint, and Judge Rascover speaks to Tobias as follows:

'Step closer to the bench,' Judge Rascover says. 'I wish to see for myself just what kind of a villain you are.'

Well, Tobias takes a step forward, and over he goes on his snoot, so I see right away what it is makes him keel over in Good Time Charley's joint, not figuring in Charley's liquor. The little guy is naturally top-heavy from the rods.

Now there is much confusion as he falls and a young doll who seems to be fatter than somewhat comes shoving through the crowd in the courtroom yelling and crying, and though the gendarmes try to stop her she gets to Tobias and kneels at his side, and speaks as follows:

'Toby, darling,' she says, 'it is nobody but Deborah who loves you dearly, and who always knows you will turn out to be the greatest gunman of them all. Look at me, Toby,' she says, 'and tell me you love me, too. We never realize what a hero you are until we get the New York papers in Erasmus last night, and I hurry to you as quickly as possible. Kiss me, Toby,' the fat young doll says, and Tobias raises up on one elbow and does same, and it makes a very pleasing scene, indeed, although the gendarmes try to pull them apart, having no patience whatever with such matters.

Now Judge Rascover is watching all this business through his specs, and Judge Rascover is no sucker, but a pretty slick old codger for a judge, and he can see that there is something wrong somewhere about Tobias Tweeney being a character as desperate as the gendarmes make him out, especially when he sees that Tobias cannot pack all these rods on a bet.

So when the gendarmes pick the fat young doll off of Tobias and take a few pounds of rods off of Tobias, too, so he is finally able to get back on his pins and stand there, Judge Rascover adjourns court, and takes Tobias into his private room and has a talk with him, and the chances are Tobias tells him the truth, for the next thing anybody knows Tobias is walking away as free as the little birdies in the trees, except that he has the fat young doll clinging to him like a porous plaster, so maybe Tobias is not so free, at that.

Well, this is about all there is to the story, except that there is afterwards plenty of heat between the parties who are present in Good Time Charley's joint when Tobias is collared, because it seems that the meeting they all attend before going to Charley's is supposed to be a peace meeting of some kind and nobody is supposed to carry any rods to this meeting just to prove their confidence in each other, so everybody is very indignant when it comes out that nobody has any confidence in anybody else at the meeting.

I never hear of Tobias Tweeney but once after all this, and it is some months afterwards when Joey Uptown and Little Mitzi are over in Pennsylvania inspecting a brewery proposition, and finding themselves near the town that is called Erasmus, they decide it will be a nice thing to drop in on Tobias Tweeney and see how he is getting along.

Well, it seems Tobias is all married up to Miss Deborah Weems, and is getting along first class, as it seems the town elects him constable, because it feels that a guy with such a desperate reputation as Tobias Tweeney's is bound to make wrongdoers keep away from Erasmus if he is an officer of the law, and Tobias's first official act is to chase Joe Trivett out of town.

But along Broadway Tobias Tweeney will always be considered nothing but an ingrate for heaving Joey Uptown and Little Mitzi into the town sneezer and getting them fined fifty bobs apiece for carrying concealed weapons.